# SEALED WITH HONOR

## A CHRISTIAN K9 ROMANTIC SUSPENSE

LAURA SCOTT

# CHAPTER ONE

Retired Navy SEAL Kaleb Tyson knelt in the shadows with his black lab, Sierra, at his side. The dog provided a sense of calm as he studied the building the slim, petite, dark-haired woman had entered.

The structure was plain and appeared abandoned, yet he knew it wasn't. He'd followed Charlotte Cambridge, a big name for such a tiny woman, to this location twice now, and what little intel he'd gathered made him believe the place was a safe house for battered women and children.

A guy like him wouldn't be welcome, and the last thing he wanted was to frighten any of the residents who had a right to their safety and privacy. But after weeks of digging into the last phone call Ava Rampart had made before she'd disappeared, he finally had something solid to go on.

Ava, the younger sister of their SEAL teammate Jaydon, had been missing for just over a month. Jaydon hadn't survived their last mission, and they'd brought his body home for a proper burial. The SEAL motto was *no man left behind.*

Dead or alive, they brought their teammates home.

Their team leader, Senior Chief Mason Gray, had taken the loss personally, but Kaleb knew they'd done their best. It wasn't anyone's fault the op had gone sideways, especially since the rest of the team had barely escaped with their lives. And had sustained the injuries to prove it.

He idly rubbed his right knee, the one that had been reconstructed after that mission. A total knee replacement at forty years old didn't bode well for his future. A bum knee and night terrors were his personal souvenirs from that op. Sierra helped keep him grounded, which was how he found himself hiding in the shadows outside a safe house located in a low-income area of Los Angeles, California.

When Kaleb glimpsed a man approaching the building, all his senses went on alert. Staying in the shadows, he pulled his Sig Sauer from its holster. Sierra kept pace at his side as he lightly ran along the edge of the building to approach the stranger from behind. His knee twinged, but he ignored it, focused on the perp in front of him. Like him, the guy was dressed in black from head to toe.

Unlike him, though, the guy wore an ugly expression on his face and seemed intent on causing trouble. Kaleb didn't know for sure if the guy was armed, but he didn't discount the possibility.

Sierra wasn't a fully trained K9 yet, but thankfully, she didn't bark much. He'd worked with her often enough over these past few months that she understood basic hand signal commands. Kaleb dropped to a crouch twenty feet behind the guy and gave her a quick hand signal. Sierra sat beside him.

Adjusting to life as a civilian hadn't been easy. Unfortunately, he couldn't just shoot at the guy, so he waited and watched.

The moment he saw the guy aim a gun at the door, Kaleb jumped to his feet. "Hey! Stop!"

A loud report echoed as the bullet entered the doorjamb. Then the guy spun and ran. Kaleb grimaced and took off after him, praying his knee would hold up. The guy had a head start, disappearing behind another building.

By the time Kaleb reached it, there was no sign of him. He scanned the area, feeling certain the guy wasn't too far away. Then he thought about the safe house being breached and turned back.

The women and children would be vulnerable to another attack now that the doorjamb had been shattered. What if that guy had an accomplice? Not good. As he approached, he slowed when he saw the dark-haired woman standing in the doorway.

Even more surprising was the gun she held in her right hand.

The image of the tiny woman holding the gun almost made him want to smile. He didn't. Instead, he holstered his own weapon and raised his hands. "Ms. Cambridge? My name is Kaleb Tyson, and I'm a friend of Ava Rampart's brother. I saw the man who tried to break in and ran after him, but unfortunately, I lost him."

Charlotte Cambridge stared at him, keeping her weapon aimed at the center of his chest. "I've called the police."

"Good, that's smart." Kaleb nodded. Sierra lifted her nose to sniff the air. "I'm not here to harm anyone, I'm looking for Ava. She's missing, and her family is worried about her."

"Ava's not here." Charlotte didn't so much as waver in her stance. "You best be on your way before the cops arrive."

"Okay, except I saw the guy who shot at your door." He kept his tone low-key and reasonable. "I'm happy to tell the police what I know."

"That's up to you." She looked as if she didn't care what happened to him. "I hope you have a permit for that gun."

"I do." Again, he wanted to grin. She looked like a tiny dynamo standing there, lecturing him on gun safety while holding him at gunpoint. "The guy who tried to get inside was roughly six feet tall, dark hair, and clean-shaven. He wore a black jacket and black jeans. The gun was a thirty-eight, I believe, although I can't say for certain." Good thing his Sig Sauer wouldn't be a match to the bullet they would dig out of the door.

"Why are you still here?" Charlotte asked, showing a tinge of annoyance.

"I told you, I'm looking for Ava Rampart. Her brother, Jaydon, was a member of our SEAL team."

"Was?"

Regret creased his features. "He didn't make it through our last op."

Charlotte surprised him by nodding. "Yeah, she mentioned that."

"So, Ava was here at one point." Finally, some common ground. The wail of sirens grew louder now, and he glanced over his shoulder, expecting them to careen around the corner any minute. "I promise I'm not a threat to you or the other women staying here. I truly just want to find Ava."

Red and blue lights flashed from two squads heading toward them. Charlotte finally lowered her weapon. "How did you know we were here?"

He swallowed hard, trying to think of a response that wouldn't alarm her. "I traced Ava's call to you, Ms. Cambridge. I must admit, it took me a while to find you."

She scowled. "It's not good that you found me at all," she snapped. Then she glanced at the damaged doorjamb. "Or that anyone else did either."

He wanted to reassure her that he hadn't given her away, but the officers approached from their respective squads, holding their weapons aimed at him. "Are you Charlotte Cambridge? Did you report gunfire?"

"Yes," she admitted.

"I'm a witness," Kaleb added calmly. "My name is Kaleb Tyson, and I'm a retired Navy SEAL. This is my K9 partner, Sierra." He used his chin to point at the dog since he still held his hands in the air. "I saw a white guy approach the door and then fire a weapon at the door handle. I shouted at him to stop, but he took off. Sierra and I followed, but unfortunately, we lost him." He glanced at Charlotte. "I didn't go too far because I was worried about the security breach putting the residents in danger. I had no way of knowing if there was a second guy hiding in the wings."

A hint of appreciation flashed across Charlotte's features before she turned toward the officers. "I reported a man following me a few days ago," she informed them. "I spoke to a Detective Karl Grimes."

"And you're sure it's not this guy?" One of the officers gestured to him.

"I'm sure. The man following me has dark hair, not blond."

"Who is he?" Kaleb asked with a frown. "An ex-husband or boyfriend?"

Charlotte shrugged. "Probably, but no one I know. Likely an ex of one of the women seeking shelter here." Her expression turned grim. "I'm not happy this safe house has been compromised."

One of the cops patted him down, took his Sig and his MK 3 knife, then asked to see his driver's license and gun permit. He handed them over, and the officer eyed them for a moment. "Kaleb with a K?"

"Yes." He got that response a lot.

"Hmm." The officer took them back to the squad, no doubt to run a background check.

He wasn't worried, considering he'd spent the past twenty-two years in the navy, there hadn't been any time to get into trouble with the law. However, he was concerned about Charlotte's safe house. "I'm happy to stick around to keep an eye on things."

She lifted a brow. "No men allowed inside."

He met her gaze squarely. "I didn't say anything about staying inside. Sierra and I can protect the place from out here."

She looked surprised at his offer but didn't say anything as another officer examined the door. "The slug is embedded in the door frame. We'll have our crime scene techs dig it out and send it for evidence."

"Thank you," Charlotte murmured.

"You're clear," the cop said as he returned with Kaleb's license and permit. "Thanks for your service to our country."

"Ah, you're welcome." He appreciated the sentiment, but he was always caught off guard when someone said that to him. Especially after that last mission had gone so wrong. Jaydon was the one who'd given the ultimate sacrifice.

More reason for them to find his younger sister, Ava.

Which brought him back to Charlotte. She'd already admitted Ava had spent time there, but he needed more. He wanted to know everything Ava had said and done while she'd been there.

Charlotte Cambridge wouldn't like it, but he wasn't going anywhere. Not until he had answers.

And not until he'd ensured her safety and that of the other women inside from whoever had shot at the safe house with the intent to get inside to harm them.

---

THE TALL HANDSOME man wasn't the guy who'd followed her before, but that didn't mean Charlotte didn't find him alarming.

She'd come a long way from those days she'd been a resident at a safe house much like the one she currently operated, but there were times she still felt vulnerable.

Kaleb—with a K—Tyson was a large, imposing man. Granted, he'd been nothing but respectful and forthright from the moment she'd spotted him, but she knew all too well that looks and actions could be deceiving.

Hadn't Jerry been sweet and considerate at first? Charming beyond belief, until the moment he'd punched her in the face. Only to turn around and claim it was her fault.

No. Charlotte gave herself a mental shake. This wasn't the time to traipse down memory lane. There was no point in reliving the past. She'd need all her energy to deal with this new threat.

The dark-haired man Kaleb had described sounded like the guy she'd glimpsed following her a few days ago. Obviously, there was no way to know for sure, but the fact that a dark-haired man had shot at the door to the safe house, likely intending to enter, was too much of a coincidence.

Swallowing a wave of helplessness, she focused on what needed to be done. There were ten women and four children inside who deserved to be safe. She could try to fix the broken door, but what if the dark-haired guy showed up again later?

Her gaze darted toward Kaleb. He'd offered to stand guard, remaining outside the building despite the cold weather. Not that winter in Los Angeles was anything like where she'd grown up in Minnesota. Still, she believed he'd meant what he'd said. That he'd stay outside to protect them.

"What's going on?"

Charlotte turned to see Milly, their live-in housekeeper, hovering behind her. Milly was only about ten years Charlotte's senior, roughly forty-seven, but she took on a motherly role to her and their residents.

"The police are here, we're fine. Nothing to be concerned about." She did her best to reassure Milly.

"Did they catch the man who shot at us?" Milly planted her hands on her plump hips.

"Not yet." Considering they didn't have much of a description to go on, Charlotte doubted they would find him anytime soon. Unless, of course, he showed up again. "Please keep everyone calm, okay? We're safe."

"Are we?" Milly stared at her for a moment before turning away. "I know the drill," she muttered as she returned to the main living quarters.

Charlotte let out a sigh. She couldn't blame Milly or the others for being afraid. She'd done everything possible to avoid being followed here, but it must not have been enough.

Why couldn't these men just leave them alone? As if it wasn't enough to terrorize women and children once, but to keep looking for them after they were gone? She didn't understand the mentality of these guys who risked everything to seek revenge.

"Ms. Cambridge?" She swung around to face Kaleb, who'd managed to approach so silently she hadn't heard him. She put a hand on her chest to calm her racing heart. "Will you allow me to fix your door?"

Far be it for her to turn down a helping hand. She glanced at his black dog, then back at him. "I have a toolbox and supplies inside. If you wouldn't mind waiting out here?"

"Yes, ma'am."

"Call me Charlotte." She was thirty-seven years old, feeling more like seventy-seven without the added ma'ams and Ms. Cambridges. Besides, she believed he was honestly here out of concern for Ava. A fear she privately shared, especially after Ava disappeared from the safe house without telling her or Milly where she was going.

Something she'd have to let Kaleb know, sooner rather than later. But not until the door was repaired.

Charlotte whirled away to get what he'd need. She returned with the toolbox and extra two-by-fours.

"Thank you." Kaleb had a flashlight out and was examining the door frame. "I can see why he used a gun, no way to get inside otherwise."

"That's the point." She crossed her arms over her chest, chilled from the cool night air.

"Do you have cameras?" Kaleb stepped back to look above the door frame.

"No," she admitted. "This is generally a temporary housing location. Residents stay only for a couple of weeks before being handed off to another location."

"You need cameras." He moved to the side to make

room for the crime scene tech. "You need motion sensor lights too."

She stared at him for a moment. "We bring victims here during the night and would prefer not to announce our location, so no lights. Besides, the outside of the building is supposed to look abandoned, not wired for sound."

"They have really small cameras, I can mount them out of view." He scanned the building. "I get your point about the lights, but I still think it's better to have them than not. Especially now."

She tried not to feel depressed. "We'll have to find a new location soon anyway, so there's no point in doing all of that." The idea of moving was daunting, although it wasn't the first time.

And it probably wouldn't be the last.

"Got it." The crime scene tech held up the slug with a triumphant look. "Mangled pretty bad, but I'd say it's a thirty-eight."

She nodded. Her gun was a small .38 as well. She practiced shooting targets every two weeks and had gotten very good. Her instructor had warned her, though, that shooting at paper silhouettes was very different from aiming and firing at a person. Still, she knew she would do whatever was necessary to keep these women safe.

The officers left shortly after the crime scene tech had gotten their evidence, leaving her and Kaleb alone.

"This won't take long." He hefted the two-by-four into place.

She stepped back to give him room to work. He seemed to know what he was doing, and soon the door was repaired so that it would close properly.

"We'll need to replace the handle and lock, but that will need to wait until morning." Kaleb pushed the toolbox inside. "Don't worry, though, I'll stay out here with Sierra. We won't let anyone get close."

"You can't stay out there all night," she protested.

He arched a brow. "I'll be fine for another eight to nine hours."

It was already midnight, and Charlotte knew she should just let him stay outside as promised. But she couldn't do it. "It's too cold. You can stay inside, but only in the hallway."

"I don't want to cause anxiety for your residents." He glanced at his dog. "Sierra and I can huddle together to stay warm."

"Please, Kaleb. I'll just worry about you out here." She glanced over her shoulder. "I'll reassure our residents, and as long as you stay in the hallway, they should be fine."

A grin tugged at the corner of his mouth. "It's sweet that you're worried, but I've stayed in far worse conditions. And out here, I can see the threat coming before it arrives." He hesitated, then added, "I wouldn't say no to a cup of coffee, though, if it's not too much trouble."

She realized he wasn't kidding about staying outside in the cold. Slowly, she nodded. "No trouble at all. Give me a few minutes to brew a pot, okay?"

"Thanks." His grin widened, and she had to look away from his ridiculously handsome features.

The man no doubt had dozens of women who'd chased after him all his life. He wasn't wearing a wedding ring, but that didn't mean anything. Charlotte reminded herself she was immune to good-looking men. Jerry had been the best cure around.

But her stomach still knotted with awareness when she returned with a large insulated mug of coffee for him. Just handing it over seemed to bring her far too close for comfort. "I—uh, should have asked if you wanted cream and sugar."

"None of that available in the Middle East," he said dryly. "Black is just fine. Thanks."

"I—um, thanks again. For doing this." She'd never felt so awkward in a man's presence as she did at that moment. Honestly, maybe she was out of practice, but still. There was no reason to overreact. It wasn't as if Kaleb was sticking around. Once he'd learned what he could about Ava's time there, he'd be on his merry way.

"Do you have a minute to talk about Ava?" He regarded her thoughtfully. "How long ago did she leave here?"

She hesitated, then decided she wouldn't be putting Ava in more danger by talking to him. The woman had left under her own free will. The safe house wasn't a jail, the women could leave if they wanted. Although once they did, they weren't allowed back to the same place. They'd have to go somewhere else.

"We're worried about her," Kaleb said when she didn't answer.

"We?"

He nodded. "The rest of Jaydon's team. Nico in particular was Jaydon's swim buddy. He's very worried about Ava and is trying to find her boyfriend, the one she supposedly left with six weeks ago."

"How many team members?" She flushed, hoping he didn't think she was being too nosy. "Never mind, I suppose that doesn't matter."

"Six of us," he replied. "Although right now, it's just me and Nico searching for Ava."

She nodded. "She left this safe house two weeks ago. I'm not sure why, she didn't confide in me. Or Milly."

"And Milly is?"

"Our live-in housekeeper, although all the women living here have chores to do. It helps to keep them busy. Idle hands and all of that. One morning we woke up, and Ava was gone, without saying a word to anyone."

"Two weeks." He sighed and rubbed the back of his neck. "If I'd have gotten here sooner . . ."

"Don't play the what-if game," she said quickly. "That's something I'm constantly preaching to the women who seek shelter here. None of us can go back and change the past, no matter how much we wish we could. All we can do is move forward."

"God's plan is not ours to question," he murmured.

She was surprised to hear him say that. Their safe house was supported financially by several Christian organizations, for which she was extremely grateful. Yet she hadn't been able to fully embrace the concept of God watching over them in the face of so many women and children suffering. "Yes, well, I—uh, should get inside. Good night."

"Good night, Charlotte." His husky voice washed over her. She turned and nearly walked face-first into the door-jamb he'd just repaired.

Feeling all kinds of foolish, she closed the door and leaned against it.

"What's wrong?" Emma, a young woman barely twenty, padded toward her. Emma had just come to the safe house three nights ago, and she was still adjusting to the routine. "Milly said we're safe, but you look worried."

She pushed her emotions aside to smile reassuringly at Emma. "We are safe, I promise. We have a bodyguard stationed outside to watch over us."

"A bodyguard?" Emma repeated, her gaze darting from Charlotte to the door behind her. "Who is he? Can we trust him?"

It broke Charlotte's heart that these women had lost their ability to trust anyone, especially men. Between drug and alcohol abuse, and general unhappiness with their lives, too many men had taken their anger and frustration out on those they were supposed to protect the most. Their women and children.

The violence never ceased to confound her, even though she'd experienced it firsthand. "Yes, Emma, we can trust him. Our bodyguard served our country as a Navy SEAL. He'll protect us tonight. And tomorrow, I'll make arrangements to move us to a new location."

Emma looked interested for a moment before turning away. Charlotte watched the young woman return to the living area, then let out a soundless sigh.

She'd truly believed they were safe here for what was left of the night.

It was only after Kaleb left that they'd have to worry about the dark-haired man finding them again.

## CHAPTER TWO

Kaleb hunkered down in the shadows with Sierra at his side. The dog sprawled across his lap, which kept him warm enough. The ground was hard and cold beneath his backside, but he ignored the discomfort as he sipped his coffee.

He thought about what Charlotte had said about needing to relocate. It sounded as if it was something they'd done before, which shouldn't have been necessary. He knew he hadn't been followed, yet following her hadn't been that difficult.

Clearly, the dark-haired guy had done that too.

Kaleb almost hoped the guy would show up again. This time, he wouldn't hesitate to give chase, especially now that he knew the little pixie was packing heat. The way she'd held the weapon had convinced him she knew how to use it.

He silently prayed she'd never have to.

The night slipped past, hour by hour. He walked with Sierra to stay awake. He scouted his surroundings, making sure there were no hidden surprises. The safe house location was perfect, and if not for his following Charlotte, he likely wouldn't have found it.

By morning, his bum knee hurt like crazy, the cold dampness not helping his newly constructed joint one bit. On the bright side, he hadn't slept and therefore hadn't suffered any nightmares or severe headaches.

He'd take the small blessings.

Charlotte opened the door and peered out at him. "You're still here."

He frowned. "Of course, what did you expect? I promised to stay."

"I know, it's just—you must be freezing. And probably need to use the bathroom."

"It's not that cold," he protested, despite his aching knee. "But I wouldn't mind taking you up on the bathroom break."

"Come inside, then." She opened the door wider to provide access. "Thankfully, everyone is still asleep."

He took that to mean he should get in and out as quickly as possible. After stepping across the threshold, he handed her the empty coffee mug and gave Sierra the hand signal to sit, then added, "Guard."

"She can do that?" Charlotte asked.

"Yeah. I've been working with her over the past few months."

"This way." She led him down the hall and gestured to a small bathroom. When he emerged a few minutes later, she handed him the mug back. "Fresh coffee."

"Thanks. As soon as the stores open, I'll head out to buy a replacement door handle." He turned to head back outside.

"Wait." The pixie surprised him by putting a hand on his arm. "I'll make you something for breakfast. I'm not the cook Milly is, but I can make eggs."

He looked down at her. This close, he could see that her

eyes were a deep aquamarine framed by dark lashes. She wore her dark hair short, which suited her dainty features. But then he frowned when he noticed a thin white scar near the corner of her right eye. He had to resist the urge to trace it with his finger. "You don't have to cook for me," he managed. "I'll have to head back to the motel at some point to feed Sierra anyway."

She glanced at the dog, still sitting tall in front of the door. "I don't have any dog food, sorry."

"I didn't expect you to," he responded.

"How do you like your eggs?" she asked. "Sunny-side up or scrambled? If I try anything fancier, you'll be disappointed."

Her wry humor made him smile. "Scrambled works great, please. And thanks."

"I'm the one who is thankful for you standing guard all night." She turned back to the kitchen. "Take a chair and sit near the door with your dog. No need to stay outside. I'm sure if that guy was planning to come back, he'd have shown up by now."

Since he agreed with her assessment, he acquiesced. Watching her work in the small kitchen made him remember his brief, ill-fated marriage. Blanche had been beautiful, and things had been great when he was home. But she had been woefully underwhelmed with what it was truly like being married to a SEAL. When he'd returned after a deployment, he'd found a brief note on top of a stack of divorce papers on the kitchen table.

*I need a man who will be there for me. Sign these and send them back to the lawyer, Blanche.*

Kaleb would have given his life for Blanche, but he also knew he couldn't do squat for her while he was deployed overseas. Which was more often than not.

He'd considered finding her and begging her to try again but realized nothing would change. He was in the navy for the long haul, so he signed the papers and sent them back. And just like that, his two-year marriage was over.

As if it had never been.

From that point forward, he'd kept his relationships short and sweet. Here today, gone tomorrow. No strings, just good times.

"Kaleb?" Charlotte was looking at him oddly. He realized he'd missed whatever she'd said.

"Sorry, zoned out for a minute."

"That's because you were awake all night." She waved the spatula at him. "I asked if you wanted toast too."

"That would be great." He shook off the remnants of the past. "Do you really have to move?"

Charlotte didn't answer for a long moment. "We should, yes. But it won't happen quickly. Finding a good location, getting the appropriate funding takes time. If the police catch this guy in the next twenty-four to forty-eight hours, then we could stay." She glanced over her shoulder at him. "But you and I both know that's not likely."

"I know I wasn't followed, Charlotte," he said. "And that guy was pretty surprised to hear me shout at him."

Her aquamarine eyes widened. "Me? You think he followed me?"

"Yes." He wouldn't lie to her. "The same way I did."

She flushed and shook her head. "I tried so hard to avoid that. Only to have failed, twice."

"In all fairness, I'm pretty good at what I do." SEALs were known for their stealth. "You reported the guy following you to the police? A Detective Grimes?"

"I did." The toast popped, so she smeared it with butter

and put it on the plate along with a pile of scrambled eggs. She brought it over to him. "I thought I lost him on the subway."

"That was a smart move." He dug in to his meal with enthusiasm.

"One that didn't work," she said with a sigh.

He hoped that didn't mean the dark-haired guy had an accomplice. He ate in silence, hoping to finish up before any of the residents woke up.

A plump woman with choppy brown hair streaked with gray came into the kitchen. She nearly shrieked when she saw him, putting a hand over her heart. "You scared me to death," she accused.

"Milly, this is Kaleb Tyson, he and his dog, Sierra, stood guard outside the safe house all night."

"You let him inside?" Milly asked in astonishment. "You never do that."

"He deserves something to eat after what he did for us." Charlotte eyed the woman. "You have a problem with that?"

"Me? No. But some of the others are skittish . . ." Milly's voice trailed off as she nudged Charlotte away from the stove.

"I'm leaving soon." Kaleb took a bite of his toast. "And I'm happy to sit outside, if needed."

"You're fine for a few more minutes," Charlotte reassured him. "We are in your debt, Kaleb."

"Not at all. I offered and don't need anything in return." In fact, he preferred it that way. "Anything else you can tell me about Ava? Or her boyfriend? I'm assuming the guy hit her if she ended up here."

Milly eyed him suspiciously. "Why are you looking for Ava?"

"He's a SEAL teammate of Jaydon's," Charlotte explained quickly. "And yes, Simon hit her several times. When she landed in the hospital with a concussion, we were notified. I went to pick her up and brought her here."

"Simon have a last name?" he asked.

"Simon Marks," Milly answered. "Ava pressed charges against him, but they let him out on bail." The woman sniffed. "As if that helps the situation any."

The last name Nico had been given was something different, a Simon Normandy, not Marks. He pulled out his phone and shot his teammate a text. *New intel on Simon, last name Marks?*

There was no immediate response. Either Nico was sleeping or he was following a hot lead.

Kaleb quickly finished his breakfast and handed his plate to Charlotte. "Thanks, I best be heading outside. The closest hardware store opens at nine o'clock. I can get the necessary supplies if you'd like."

"Thanks, but it's my responsibility." Charlotte took the plate. "I'll get what I need. You don't have to stay."

"Yeah, I do." Hearing movement from one of the rooms on the other side of the living space, he strode quickly to the door. "Come, Sierra." He stepped outside with his dog, then closed the door behind him.

He stood leaning against the building, thinking about Ava. This lead hadn't provided much information, yet every scrap of intel was better than none. Still, he didn't think sticking around would gain him anything. Ava had stayed here after suffering a concussion, but then she had taken off without telling anyone.

Leaving no hint behind as to where she may have gone.

Absently rubbing his aching knee, Kaleb thought about

his next steps. Without anything other than the boyfriend's name, he had no idea where to look.

Besides, he couldn't just walk away. Not now. It wasn't in his DNA to leave a group of women alone and vulnerable.

Charlotte needed help. At least for a couple of days. Maybe he could set a trap for the dark-haired guy so that Charlotte and her residents wouldn't be forced into moving to a new and secure location.

Kaleb glanced down at Sierra. "I see many more hours of sitting outside in our future, girl," he said.

Sierra licked his fingers in agreement.

Charlotte emerged from the safe house at a quarter to nine. He pushed away from the wall. "I hate that you're going alone. Please let me get the supplies for you."

She hesitated. "It's better to have you remain here to keep an eye on the safe house until I get back."

"I don't mind, and I'm pretty sure you're just as armed and dangerous," he pointed out.

A smile tugged at the corner of her mouth. "I left my gun with Milly. We both have permits and practice every two weeks."

He could tell he wasn't going to be able to sway her, so he nodded. "Okay, but be safe. I can pick up the cameras later if you are able to stay. Oh, and take my phone number in case you need something."

"Okay," she agreed.

After they exchanged phone numbers, she left, walking at a brisk pace. He stared for a moment at the number he'd added to his contact list, with her name above it.

Why did he feel like he was a twenty-year-old kid scoring the pretty girl's phone number? He rolled his eyes at his own foolishness.

Time to get a grip. He was only sticking around for a few days. He didn't live in LA and had never wanted to.

Once he knew Charlotte and her residents were safe, he'd be on his way.

To what? He wasn't quite sure.

---

CHARLOTTE MADE her way down the block, resisting the urge to look back at Kaleb. What was wrong with her? First cooking for him, now wishing he'd come with her? She shook her head. Just because he was one of the nicest guys she'd met in what seemed like forever didn't mean she should allow herself to get too close.

Kaleb was only here because of Ava. And the moment she had the door repaired, he'd leave to continue searching for the missing woman.

She admired Kaleb for his determination to find Ava. So many women disappeared, never to be heard from again, and most of the time, nothing much was done about it. He seemed to be an honorable man, a rarity these days.

Well, probably not really. Charlotte knew that her view of men was skewed, first by Jerry and then by the other women she'd surrounded herself with. Women who'd learned the hard way that men who hit were always *sorry* but didn't stop.

Not without a lot of counseling or prison time. Often both.

Jerry had been arrested, and she'd pressed charges against him the first time he'd hit her. Unfortunately, he hadn't done much time, and when he'd gotten out of jail, he'd found her again. That assault had been the last straw. After waking up in the hospital, she'd skedaddled out of

Minneapolis, making her way across the country to finally end up here in Los Angeles.

Last time she'd looked him up, Jerry had pictures online boasting of his recent marriage to a woman by the name of Darla. A woman she felt sorry for as she knew it was only a matter of time before Jerry took his anger out on her too.

Keeping a keen eye out for the dark-haired man, Charlotte crossed the street and turned left. She knew where the closest hardware store was located as she'd been there before. One of her residents had lost it one night shortly after Ava had left and punched a hole in the wall. Charlotte had gone to buy plaster and paint to repair the damage.

Normally the women and children who came to stay didn't lash out in violence, but this had been a rare exception. Charlotte had insisted Jane get intensive counseling or leave.

Jane had chosen to leave.

It was difficult to let go. Charlotte knew that Jane would ultimately end up in another abusive relationship. It was a pattern she'd witnessed before. She and the social workers who referred clients did good work and had saved many women and children from harm or worse, death, by providing them safety and security.

Along with the opportunity to start over.

But she couldn't save them all. Some, like Ava and Jane, refused to be saved.

After taking a long, circuitous route, Charlotte arrived at the hardware store. She stepped inside and went straight to the section of door handles. The model wasn't anything fancy, but it was the most heavy-duty door handle available. She purchased what she needed, along with new locks and keys, then prepared to walk back.

The moment she stepped out of the doorway, she

glimpsed a dark-haired man hurrying away. On reflex, she whirled and went back inside the store, her heart thudding painfully against her ribs.

The same guy as last night? Highly doubtful. The gunfire had unnerved her to the point she hadn't been able to get much sleep. Deep down, she'd assumed Kaleb had given up his watch, leaving them alone.

She drew in a deep, ragged breath. Nearly four million people lived in LA, and with the large Hispanic population, the majority had dark hair. She couldn't even say if the guy she'd glimpsed was white or Hispanic, much less match him with the man who'd followed her a few days ago.

Time to stop letting her imagination run away with her. The chances of the dark-haired man finding her at the hardware store were slim to none.

Unless, of course, he'd assumed she'd be here bright and early to fix the door he'd busted.

She shivered and patted her pocket for her phone. Then she dropped her hand. No, she wasn't going to call Kaleb. He was needed more at the safe house. While Milly did know how to use a gun and took target practice lessons, the woman was a terrible shot. And unfortunately, the housekeeper's skills hadn't improved over time.

"Can I help you with something?"

The deep voice at her elbow made her jump and stumble backward. Her cheeks flushed as she looked at the older man who stood there. "No, thank you. I'm fine."

His expression said he didn't believe her, but he moved away. Charlotte tightened her grip on the bag and resolutely pushed the door open.

She lingered outside the store, taking a moment to look both ways up and down the street. Thankfully, there wasn't a dark-haired man lurking nearby. The guy she'd seen was probably harmless. Yet, old habits died hard, so she turned left in the opposite direction from the safe house, deciding to take the subway.

Kaleb had said using the subway was a smart move. The memory of his praise gave her a warm glow. Maybe he'd been humoring her, but it couldn't hurt to deploy the same tactic again.

Moving through the city while constantly looking over her shoulder reminded her of those first few days after she'd left Jerry. The man who'd professed to love her had isolated her from her friends, making her feel alone. Then he had lashed out at her physically while blaming her for his anger.

Typical of men who are controlling. She was smart, had graduated from college with an accounting degree, but yet she'd stupidly fallen for his fake charm. And his apparent concern, which was really nothing more than a ploy to keep her under his thumb.

She hurried down to the subway station, idly fingering her closely cropped hair. Cutting it off had been symbolic and cathartic.

His first assault had been to hit her in the head with a beer bottle, causing her to need several stitches above her right eye. Jerry had accompanied her to the hospital, trying to explain that she'd hit her head on a cabinet door, but she could tell the ER doc hadn't believed him. When Jerry stepped out to get coffee, she'd explained what had happened, and they'd called the police to haul him away.

Only he hadn't stayed in jail for long. His bail had been set for a ridiculously low amount, and he'd gotten out. He'd found where she was staying and had pushed his way inside. Then he'd grabbed her by the hair, slamming her head against the kitchen counter. She'd blacked out and had woken in the hospital.

The doc had once again wanted her to press charges, but she was too afraid. The cold, angry expression in Jerry's eyes had scared her to death. What if they let him out again? She felt certain he'd find her and kill her.

So she'd left the hospital without pressing charges and had gone to a safe house in Minneapolis. After a few days, she had cleaned out her meager savings and headed west, stopping only when she needed more money.

The once brilliant accountant waitressed in truck stop cafés to earn money for the next leg of her journey. Soon, she'd stopped looking over her shoulder and had begun to feel safe and secure in her new life.

Until now.

Threading her way through the crowds, she did her best to disappear. Her slender build helped as much as it hindered. She couldn't easily see beyond the tall people around her if the dark-haired guy was nearby.

Even if he was, she was safe enough. He'd made his move late at night using a gun to bulldoze his way into the safe house.

Not likely he'd try something in broad daylight with hundreds of witnesses.

As she moved onto the subway with the others, she wondered which resident the guy was targeting. Emma was their newest addition, along with a woman named LeeAnn. Then again, Jodie Armbruster and her young daughter, Angela, had come just a few days earlier than those two. And before that was Willow and her son, Tommy.

She made a mental note to question them about their abusers. Willow had sported dozens of bruises on her chest and arms, and her six-year-old son, Tommy, had come in with a black eye.

Any man who would give a six-year-old a black eye

deserved to rot in jail for the rest of his miserable life. Too bad the penalty for child and spousal abuse wasn't as severe as she'd like.

Only when the injuries reached the level of severe bodily harm or attempted murder did the abuser get significant jail time. And even then a good lawyer often got them off without doing much except promising to go to anger management classes.

As if that helped.

Charlotte shook off her dour thoughts and got off the subway after two stops. Then she backtracked, walking to another subway stop that would take her closer to the safe house.

While sandwiched between a teenage boy and a man old enough to be her father, her phone buzzed. Easing it from her pocket, she smiled when she saw Kaleb's text. *Where r u? Everything okay?*

With a bit of jostling and tucking her bag from the hardware store beneath her arm, she was able to type back. *Fine, taking the long way home.*

*Why? Did someone scare u?*

His instincts were on right track, even though he was proving to be a bigger worrywart than Milly. *I'm fine, be there soon.*

*Ok.*

She stared at the text exchange feeling a bit foolish. At her age, thirty-seven-and-a-half and counting, she was too old to act like a high school teenager looking for a prom date. Besides, Kaleb was way out of her league.

Too handsome, too big, and too strong. Too charming.

Too—*everything*.

Shaking her head at her ridiculous thoughts, she exited

the train and hurried up to the street level. As she turned to the right, she saw him.

The dark-haired man!

Without hesitation, she ducked back into the subway station, going back down to the familiar crowds. Her palms were damp with sweat, and she had to grip the hardware store bag tighter to avoid dropping it.

Was it the same man as before? Or was she losing her mind? Had he seen her?

The train had already left, forcing her to wait for the next one. She positioned herself near a concrete post where she could watch the down escalator.

It only took a minute to see the same dark-haired man step onto the escalator. She tried to get a better look at his features, but it wasn't easy as he was moving and other much taller people kept getting in her way.

This time she knew for certain he was looking for her. He must have seen her come out of the subway station and dart back inside.

She tightened her grip on the bag containing the heavy-duty metal door handle. It wasn't a gun, but she'd use it as a weapon if needed.

When she lost sight of the dark-haired man, she eased along the other edge of the concrete pillar, keeping it between her and the stranger. His dark clothing blended in with the others too well, but she managed to see him walking past, his head swiveling from side to side as he scanned the crowd looking for her.

If he was closer, she'd swing the door handle in her bag at his head. But after he'd walked past, she decided to make a run for it. First, she shrugged out of her jacket, then eased out from behind the pillar. She hurried to catch up with two young girls chatting about boys.

"Excuse me, do you know which way Duncan Street is?" She leaned forward, wedging herself between them to make it appear as if the three of them were traveling together.

Or so she hoped.

"Um, yeah, I think it's a couple of blocks to the right," the one girl said. The other one looked at her strangely as if wondering why she was invading their personal space.

"Thanks, I'm new to the area, and I am always getting lost." She didn't dare look back over her shoulder. The escalator seemed to move with excruciating slowness, but they finally reached the top. Charlotte stayed with the girls until they were outside on the street.

Then she began to run.

# CHAPTER THREE

The itch crawling up the back of his neck was impossible to ignore. Kaleb didn't want to leave the safe house unprotected, but he couldn't just stand there doing nothing while Charlotte was facing possible danger.

He was too far away from San Diego to call their team leader, Senior Chief Mason Gray, for help. Nico was following his own lead, and three of the guys were spread out across the country, dealing with their own issues. Hudson, his former swim buddy, had gone so far off-grid no one knew where he was.

This being a civilian and not having a fellow SEAL covering your six pretty much sucked. He was used to working as a team, not solo. He considered putting Sierra on guard and taking the chance but worried the black lab might be killed since the dark-haired guy clearly had a weapon.

Just as he was about to call the local cops, begging for one of them to come stand guard, he saw a woman running down the street toward him.

Charlotte! Shoving the phone into his pocket, he ran

forward to meet her with Sierra keeping pace at his side, wincing as his bum knee protested the sudden movement.

He lightly grasped her shoulders when she reached him. "What happened?"

"I—saw him. The dark-haired man." She was breathing heavily from the exertion. She glanced furtively over her shoulder. "I think I lost him in the subway."

He scanned the area without seeing any sign of the guy. But there was no reason for him to follow her, either, since he already knew where the safe house was located. Kaleb scowled and put his arm around her shoulders. "Let's get you inside."

"Wait. I have the replacement door handle and lock." She thrust the bag at him. "I know I'm asking a lot, but will you help install it?"

"Of course. It's not asking too much, I was planning to do it anyway." He tried to smile reassuringly. "You'll be safe now."

She let out a sound that was half snort, half laugh. "Safe? I don't think so. Not if that guy anticipated I'd be heading to the closest hardware store first thing this morning. I thought I imagined him, until he popped up again outside the subway station."

It was a good point, and Kaleb didn't like it. "You should report this to the police."

"Yeah, okay, but they're not going to do anything since I have no idea who this guy is." She blew out a frustrated breath. "I'm sorry, I don't mean to be crabby."

"You're not." He was upset enough on her behalf. "Go reassure your residents while I get this door handle fixed, okay?"

She hovered in the doorway for a moment, then nodded. "I'll get the toolbox. Would you like coffee?"

"That would be great." He rarely turned down coffee, and brewing a pot would give her something constructive to do.

Charlotte returned with the tools, then left again. As he worked, he could hear muted voices coming from the kitchen. He suspected Charlotte wasn't the type to whine to Milly or any of the other residents about her problems, but they may be making plans to relocate.

It irked him that they had to leave what should have been a safe zone. He wasn't a violent man by nature, but he wouldn't hesitate to punch dark-haired guy if given the chance. In fact, he almost hoped the guy showed up again. This time, Kaleb would make sure to take him down.

He caught Charlotte's flowery scent. Glancing over his shoulder, he saw her approaching with the same insulated mug of coffee. "Here you go."

"Thanks." He took a grateful sip, then set the mug on the floor, well out of the way of his workspace. "Didn't you say something about a Detective Grimes?"

"Yes." She shrugged. "I'll give him another call, although I would have thought he'd contact me after getting the report on the gunfire last night."

"I'm sure it takes time for paperwork to make its way through the system." He was all too familiar with government bureaucracy. The way he'd had to wait to get his knee replaced for the appropriate paperwork proving he'd been injured during their last op proved that. "Call him. I'm sure he'll want to know about both events."

She nodded slowly, then turned away.

The door repair took less than an hour. Yet even though he was satisfied that it was sturdy enough, nothing would stop a bullet. The way the perp had shot at the right spot in the doorjamb to bypass the lock was concerning. Sierra sat looking up at him expectantly, and he knew he needed to feed her very soon.

Which meant leaving the safe house for at least forty-five minutes, maybe longer.

He replaced the tools and clicked the box shut. Then he stood for a moment, debating whether to enter the safe house inner sanctuary. Pushing the box off to the side, he opened the door to step outside.

"Kaleb?" Charlotte hurried toward him. "I—um, wanted to tell you that Detective Grimes will be here in thirty minutes. He wanted to talk to you about your version of events, if you can spare the time."

"I don't mind hanging around, although I will need to feed Sierra soon."

"Oh, I see." She frowned. "You know, there's a pet supply store that isn't too far away. I'm happy to pay for a small bag of dog food for Sierra."

"It's not a matter of paying, I have plenty of money, but I don't want to leave you and the others here alone. Especially since you saw the dark-haired guy recently. I wouldn't put it past him to come back."

"I'm armed," she reminded him. "And honestly, you can't just stand out here all day. I'm sure you have someplace to go. You're still searching for Ava, right?"

"Yes." Although this particular lead had pretty much become a dead end.

"Besides, I don't want to waste your time. It's more likely he'll try to come again at night."

"Maybe." Her assessment was the more likely scenario. "You didn't get any cameras."

"No." She lifted her hands helplessly. "No point, we

need to move. I'm waiting to hear back from my largest charity donor to see if she'll help foot the bill."

He was glad she had generous donors, yet being at their mercy must be difficult. "And if she doesn't?"

Charlotte hesitated, then shrugged, her attempt to smile falling flat. "We'll find a way. We always do."

Kaleb hated feeling so helpless. He could certainly donate what cash he had on him, and his time, but that wouldn't be enough for the long haul. And he really needed to call Nico to let him know that Ava had been at the safe house but wasn't any longer.

If Jaydon were alive, he'd expect his teammates to help find his sister. The fact that Jay hadn't survived didn't change those expectations. His being dead only added to their need to step up.

Finding Ava was the least they could do. Sticking around LA wasn't likely to help him do that. It was a big city, but something must have spooked Ava into leaving, and it didn't make sense that she'd stick around in the same place.

"Really, Kaleb, it's okay." Charlotte reached out to touch his arm, the warmth of her fingers giving him a little zing. "I totally understand this isn't your problem. You've done more than your fair share already. Not just spending the night outside but in serving our country."

He stared at her, wishing he could sweep her into his arms for a kiss. But, of course, he couldn't. She wouldn't welcome that from him, and the last thing he wanted was to make her uncomfortable.

It took a moment for him to control his emotions enough to respond. "It's not enough, but it's a start. I'll stay until Grimes gets here, then run and grab the dog food for Sierra. That way, you won't be alone while I'm gone."

She frowned. "Kaleb, you can't sit here all day. You need to sleep."

"Sleep is overrated." His attempt at humor only made her scowl deepen. He sighed and added, "I'll think of something."

Shaking her head, she turned away. He watched her go, thinking again about how tiny she was to be doing something as dangerous as this. He didn't know her story, but it didn't take a genius to figure out she must have once been a resident in a safe house like this. The thought of a man hitting someone as petite as Charlotte brought a wave of red-hot fury.

During his multiple tours overseas, he'd witnessed too many horrific acts of violence. Thankfully, he had been able to take out many a bad guy responsible for the terror. At times, it seemed as if they were playing a game of whack-a-mole where the moment you got rid of one tango, another took his place. Over the years, though, he'd seen some progress, enough to keep him believing that the good guys would win.

Yet now, he was astounded to be faced with the same sort of violence happening right here at home. Crimes against women and children. Those same people men were supposed to protect.

It made him mad, but anger wouldn't help. Taking action to fight against the abuse was the only answer.

Kaleb took up his sentinel position outside the safe house door. Yeah, there was no way he'd be leaving Los Angeles anytime soon.

Not until Charlotte and the other residents were safe.

Twenty minutes later, Detective Karl Grimes showed up. He looked to be the same age as Kaleb, early forties, although he carried a bit of paunch around his belly.

"Are you Kaleb Tyson?" Grimes asked.

"Yes, sir." Kaleb held out his hand, and the detective looked surprised as he took it. "Thanks for coming."

"I understand you were here last night and witnessed the guy shooting at the safe house?"

He nodded. "I did, yes. I shouted at him to stop, which made him take off. Sierra and I gave chase, but he disappeared out of sight. I'm not that familiar with the city and didn't want to leave the women unattended, so I came back."

Grimes looked from him to Sierra and back again. "Retired Navy SEAL?"

"Yes, sir." He felt as if he were talking to a senior officer. "I came here specifically to talk to Ms. Cambridge about one of her residents, Ava Rampart. She's missing."

"And that's a job for a retired SEAL?" Grimes asked, raising his brow.

"She's the sister of a fallen teammate." Kaleb shifted his weight off his bum knee, wishing the third degree would end soon. "We're just trying to help, that's all."

"Sometimes helping gets in the way," Grimes pointed out.

Kaleb bit his lip to stop from snapping back. "Maybe. But the local police don't have any leads and aren't really searching for her as it appears she willingly left with her boyfriend. We're not stepping on any toes, sir."

Grimes stared a moment longer, then nodded. "I guess it can't hurt. Not my case, either way. Just curious how you found this safe house."

Kaleb knew he was treading on thin ice. The buddy who'd helped him out hadn't gone through legit channels to get the phone call information. "We traced one of Ava's last calls to Ms. Cambridge. I found and followed her here. The same way the dark-haired guy must have done."

"We?" Grimes asked, then waved a hand. "Never mind. I probably don't want to know."

Kaleb didn't respond.

"Did you get a good look at the shooter's face?" Grimes asked.

"Just a flash, sorry." He repeated verbatim what he'd told the officers the night before. "Ms. Cambridge saw him again today, so she likely has more information to share."

"I heard." Grimes lifted his fist to pound on the door. Moments later, Charlotte opened it.

The moment the detective disappeared inside, Kaleb sprang into action. He didn't know how long the detective would stick around, so the sooner he grabbed dog food for Sierra, the better. He'd already pulled up the pet supply store on his phone, and the map app informed him the place was twelve minutes away.

He made it in eight, with Sierra running with glee beside him. She was only two years old and still had plenty of energy. Staying outside all night hadn't seemed to hurt her any, which was a relief.

After purchasing the food, he ran back to the safe house. His knee held up fairly well, thankfully the joint loosened up as he ran. The surgeon at the Veteran's Administration Hospital had told him that staying active was the best way to keep the knee working well, as long as he didn't overdo it by running marathons.

Kaleb hoped and prayed he was right about that.

Grimes was just leaving as Kaleb and Sierra returned. He grinned and gave himself a mental high five for making it back in time.

"I'll get you two bowls for Sierra," Charlotte said when he set the bag of food down. "I'm sure she needs water too."

"Thanks." He nodded at the detective. "Any leads on who this guy is?"

"Nothing specific." Grimes glanced at the safe house. "Many of the women in there have ex-husbands and boyfriends, most with dark hair."

"Why not put together a photo array of their exes and see if Charlotte recognizes any of them?" he suggested.

"I'm in the process of doing that; however, a high percentage of these guys aren't in the system."

"What do you mean?" Kaleb frowned. "They must have been arrested and charged for the abuse."

"Only if the victim presses charges. And that often doesn't happen. Especially if they just want to disappear, to start over someplace new."

Kaleb grimaced, knowing he was right. Was that what Ava had done?

"I'll be back with the photos I am able to dig up." Grimes turned and walked back to his brown sedan.

Kaleb watched him leave, then turned when the door opened. Instead of holding the bowls, Charlotte was looking at him expectantly. "You can come inside."

"Ah, that's okay. I don't want to upset anyone."

A hint of a smile crossed her features. "We took a vote. The overwhelming response was to invite you in so you can get some sleep."

A vote? He lifted a brow. "You're running a democracy?"

"Yes." She gestured for him to come inside. "The women here have decided they'd like to have a bodyguard on the premises until we can be relocated. I know it's not much, but we can offer you a bed and meals."

He went inside, then closed and locked the door behind him. "Did you talk them into this?"

"Not me." Her smile widened. "But Milly did."

He was humbled and honored by their trust in him. He nodded slowly and followed Charlotte into the kitchen.

Clearly, God had sent him here for two reasons. To find Ava and to keep these women safe.

He nodded to himself. Yep. Kaleb was fully on board with His plan.

---

HOPING Kaleb didn't pick up on her nervousness, Charlotte filled a bowl with water. Before she could set it on the floor, Kaleb took it from her hand, their fingers brushing.

"I've trained Sierra to only accept food and water from me," he said in an apologetic tone. "It's a way to prevent bad guys from giving her drugged or poisoned food."

"Poison?" she echoed in surprise. Although really, nothing should shock her by now. "Very smart, I completely understand."

"Thanks." He set down the water dish, filled the second bowl with food, then stepped back. Sierra sat and watched him, waiting for permission to eat.

"Go," he said, pointing at the bowls.

Instantly, Sierra stood and trotted over to the dishes, clearly hungry as she began to eat. Charlotte couldn't help being impressed. "She's really well trained."

"It's all I've been doing over the past few months," Kaleb admitted. "I'm still trying to get used to life outside the navy."

"How long did you serve?"

"Twenty-two years," he answered absently as if his

thoughts were a million miles away. "When Sierra is finished, we'll take a nap."

"Sounds good." She'd given up her own bed for his use. Easier in the long run, and Milly had already changed the bedding. "Again, we appreciate you staying."

"I offered." He finally turned to look at her. His brown eyes held compassion. "I was thinking a mattress in front of the door would work."

"Really? Isn't that a bit extreme?"

"Easier for me to protect you near the doorway. He could get all the way inside if I'm off in some other room." He glanced around. "I noticed there's a row of high windows in the living room."

"Uh, yeah. We needed some natural light. But we purposefully kept them high off the ground to prevent anyone from easily crawling inside."

He nodded. "I figured."

"I'll grab the mattress." She turned to leave, but he quickly stopped her.

"No, I'll get it. Just give me a few minutes. Trust me, it doesn't take Sierra long to eat."

"Char?" A female voice from the doorway between the kitchen and living area had her turning to face Emma. "I—uh, it's my turn to do dishes, right?"

"Yes, we'll be out of your way soon." Since Emma never jumped to do chores, Charlotte knew the real reason the woman had ventured into the kitchen was to get an up close and personal look at Kaleb. Emma was young and balked at some of the rules. Before coming to the shelter, the girl had gone to various clubs at night, chafing at the restrictions Charlotte enforced at the safe house.

"You must be Kaleb." Emma smiled and swayed her

hips as she came farther into the room. "I'm Emma Yonkers. It's nice to meet you."

"Ma'am." Kaleb gave her a reserved nod. If he noticed the young woman flirting, he didn't show it. "Sierra and I will be out of your way soon."

"Oh, you're fine. I love dogs." Emma barely glanced at Sierra. "I don't mind company while I work."

Charlotte barely refrained from rolling her eyes. "Mr. Tyson needs to sleep. He and Sierra stayed awake all night to protect us. I'm sure he doesn't want us bothering him."

Emma flushed and shrugged. "I'm sorry, Kaleb. I don't mean to be a bother."

"You're not. But we are going to get some sleep." He was nothing but respectful to Emma, which only made Charlotte admire him more.

Emma was curvy and beautiful, with long, wavy dark hair. For the first time in years, Charlotte wished she hadn't cut her hair. She fingered the short strands, then shook off the ridiculous thought.

Kaleb had to be in his early forties if he'd served in the navy for twenty-two years. She didn't think it likely he'd be interested in twenty-year-old Emma.

Then again, she didn't seem to know much about what men did or didn't like.

Whoa, where did that come from? What was wrong with her? This wasn't the time to wallow in self-pity. None of this was about her, it was about keeping these women and children safe.

A mission upon which she'd dedicated the past five years of her life.

Having a relationship, even a simple friendship, would be nearly impossible. She wouldn't expect anyone to jump on board with her.

No matter how tempting.

"Charlotte?" Kaleb's deep husky voice penetrated her thoughts. "Will you show me the room where I can grab the mattress?"

"Oh, you can borrow mine," Emma quickly offered. The woman had filled up the sink with hot soapy water to begin the dishes. "I don't mind."

"Thanks, but I'll take care of it." Charlotte gestured for Kaleb to follow her. "This way."

Several of the women were gathered in the living room, along with a couple of the kids. Three young girls were playing with dolls, Tommy was playing a sports video game, no violent ones allowed. They all stared at Kaleb as he walked past. She gave him credit for keeping his distance to avoid frightening them.

Moments later, he'd pulled her twin mattress through the safe house to the hallway. "Thanks, Charlotte. This is great."

"It's the least we can do." She hesitated, then added, "Emma is—young."

He grinned. "Yeah, figured that out on my own. No worries. I'm not interested."

He wasn't interested in Emma? Or women in general? Or what?

"I married young, came home from being deployed to a note and divorce papers." Kaleb shrugged. "I can't say that I blamed my wife, but it hurt all the same."

"I'm sorry to hear that." She couldn't imagine any sane woman walking away from Kaleb Tyson. Then again, she'd been engaged to an egotistical, charming narcissist, so her opinion may be a bit skewed.

"No reason to be sorry. It was amicable for the most part." He pinned her with a knowing gaze. "And I'm sure it could have been worse."

She felt naked and exposed, as if he could see all the secrets she'd buried deep inside. "Everyone's situation is different. Not better or worse. It is what it is."

"Is that how you've survived?"

"Yes." She stepped back, eager to put distance between them. "I'll let you get some sleep."

"Thanks. Come, Sierra."

Charlotte left Kaleb and Sierra on the mattress huddled beneath a thin blanket. The man unnerved her, but not necessarily in a bad way. She wasn't afraid of him.

But she was afraid of the way he made her feel. As if her life was lacking in some way.

As if she wanted, maybe even deserved, more.

Charlotte forced herself to concentrate on her next steps. First and foremost, getting funding for the move. She moved away from the living space, not wanting the residents to hear her begging for cash.

No need for them to worry.

An hour later, she set the phone aside and rubbed her temples. She'd secured some funding, but not enough. She'd already used all her own personal savings, so that wasn't an option.

The female donor who'd come through with the initial funds had promised to raise more. Charlotte grateful for whatever she could do. She kept the woman's identity a secret, as promised, because she was once married to a very prominent congressman. The man had passed away from cancer a few years ago. The woman had confided to Charlotte that her husband was terribly abusive and that was why she wanted to use as much of his money as possible to help other women escape.

Charlotte was grateful for every dollar that came in. She kept impeccable records in case they were ever audited.

She stood and returned to the living area just as several gunshots echoed from outside. The glass in the high windows along the living room wall shattered into zillions of pieces, raining on the women and children seated below.

# CHAPTER FOUR

The sound of gunfire brought Kaleb out of a sound sleep. For a moment, he thought he was in Afghanistan, then his gaze landed on the hallway of the safe house, and he remembered he was there to protect the residents staying there.

Sierra was growling, staring in the direction of the living room. He leaped up and ran down the hallway, listening as several women and children cried out in alarm. "Charlotte? Is anyone hurt?"

"Just scared." Her response wasn't easy to hear amidst the crying. "Shh, it's okay. We're fine. Let's gather in the kitchen, okay?"

He eased past the women and children who were hurrying past to seek shelter in the small kitchen. He moved into the living room. The shattered window let in a chill, and he scowled at the glass shards covering the furniture and the floor.

"I can't believe he did this." Charlotte came to stand beside him, looking pale and grim. "Not to get inside but to scare us."

"Yeah." Kaleb didn't like it. "Did you call Grimes?"

"I did. He said he'd come as soon as possible." She didn't sound overly enthused with the response, and frankly, he couldn't blame her.

"In the meantime, I'll get those two windows boarded up."

She shook her head. "He'll just shoot at the boards too. We'll need to find a new place to go as soon as possible."

"I have some money we can use," Kaleb said. "Contact your donor again. The biggest issue is that we'll need a ride, something large enough to carry sixteen people."

"We've chartered a bus in the past, but that won't help until we have a new location." Charlotte sighed. "Two of our residents were scheduled to be relocated today. There's a private car coming at noon to take them to a long-term location."

"Fourteen people, then." Kaleb glanced at her. "I'm still going to board those windows up. If nothing else, it will make your residents feel safe and provide some warmth. You came up with a two-by-four to fix the door frame, do you have plywood too?"

"Yes. I can show you." She led the way down the hallway to a room that held all sorts of building supplies.

"Why do you have all this?" He tucked tools into his pocket, a hammer, nails, and a handsaw, then picked up a small sheet of plywood. "Seems unusual."

"They made some accommodations to this space, and I asked them to leave whatever they had left over behind." Charlotte shrugged. "I knew from experience it's good to be prepared to make repairs."

"This kind of thing happens often?" He stared at her.

"Our safe houses aren't often breached, no, but damage to walls or doors from anger or frustration? Yeah."

Understandable to a certain extent. He carried everything into the living room and stared up at the high windows. "I didn't see a ladder in there."

"We have a step stool." Charlotte left the room, returning a few minutes later with a decent-sized step stool. "You're tall enough that this should work."

"Thanks." He went to work, mentally reviewing their next steps. Renting a bus wouldn't be difficult, but getting everyone out of here to another location without this guy following might be tricky. He tried to come up with an alternative location, knowing any of the larger homes able to accommodate this many people would be super expensive.

Kaleb didn't mind using his personal funds. One thing about being a Navy SEAL off on deployments for years at a time was that he hadn't spent much of his earnings.

While he boarded up the windows, Charlotte and Milly swept up the glass. He could hear the murmur of voices from the kitchen, wishing the women and children didn't have to be so frightened in a place that should have been safe.

He really wanted to get this guy. If there was a way to relocate these women and kids without tipping him off, Kaleb considered returning here to set a trap for him.

Yet he didn't want to leave Charlotte and the others alone and vulnerable in a new place either.

He decided to worry about that once they'd been relocated. When he finished covering the broken window, he put the tools away. Hearing a knock at the door, he gestured for Charlotte and Milly to stay back so that he and Sierra could answer. He set the mattress up on its side, then tentatively opened the door.

Detective Grimes appeared surprised to see him. "Tyson? What are you doing here?"

"Protecting the residents." He opened the door and gestured for the detective to come in. "Good thing, too, considering how this guy didn't wait long to strike again."

"You saw him?" Grimes asked.

"No, but who else would shoot out the windows?" Kaleb took a moment to glance around the area before closing and locking the door. He highly doubted the dark-haired guy would linger nearby, that would be too risky.

Although shooting the windows during the day had been gutsy. Almost as if he wasn't worried about getting caught.

That thought gave him pause. Did this guy have connections of some sort? Was he wealthy? Knew people in power?

He decided to talk to Charlotte about that later. For now, he stood off to the side with Sierra, listening as Charlotte and Milly spoke to Detective Grimes about the sequence of events.

Kaleb didn't have anything to add, considering he'd been zonked out when the incident had taken place. Good thing no one had gotten hurt, or he'd feel guilty. At least he'd managed to get about three hours of shut-eye, which wasn't bad.

"Take a look at these photos, let me know if anyone looks familiar." Grimes displayed two sheets of paper, each containing six mug shots.

Kaleb moved forward to look over Charlotte's shoulder. He took his time looking at each face, but he didn't recognize any of them as the guy he'd scared off the previous night.

"I'm sorry." Charlotte shook her head. "None of these men is the one I saw earlier today."

Grimes appeared disappointed. "Okay, we'll keep trying."

Kaleb wished they had something more to go on. "Are some of these men the abusers of the women here?"

"Three of them, yes." Grimes shrugged. "I'm still working on the others."

He swallowed against a surge of frustration. "We need that information soon; these women are clearly in danger."

"I'm aware of the danger, and I am doing my best." A hint of defensiveness laced Grimes's tone. "Trust me, I'm taking these attacks seriously."

"I know you are." Kaleb blew out a sigh. "We'll likely be moving somewhere else later today, but I'll give you my number so that we can keep in touch."

Grimes nodded. "I understand, that would be good, thanks." He hesitated, then added, "I'm working solo as my partner ended up in the hospital with gallbladder issues. I have access to more resources, though, if needed."

"I understand." After exchanging numbers, Kaleb escorted the detective to the door. When he turned back, he found Emma hovering in the hallway, smiling flirtatiously.

"I'm so glad you're here to keep us safe." When Emma took a step forward, he instinctively backed up. "It's nice to have a big strong man looking out for us."

He figured he was old enough to be her father, but that didn't seem to bother her much. "You're welcome, and I'm glad to be here. If you'll excuse me, I have some things to discuss with Charlotte."

Disappointment flashed across her features. "Oh, sure."

Emma reminded him so much of his first wife, Blanche, it was almost comical. He skirted around the young woman, relieved to find Charlotte in the kitchen. Milly was at the stove, cooking something that smelled delicious. His stomach rumbled, and he flushed when Charlotte glanced at him.

"You mentioned the transportation for two of your residents will be here at noon?" When she nodded, he said, "It's eleven thirty now, is there something you need from me to help with that?"

"No, Jessie and Maria are packed and ready to go." She offered a wan smile. "I'm sure after everything that's happened over the past twenty-four hours, they'll be happy to leave."

"Is there a way to move up the timeline for the other residents to be relocated?"

"No, we generally have to wait for spaces to open up." Charlotte's expression turned serious. "There are more women and children needing protection than places to house them."

"Okay, then let's find a new place to go, even for a few days." He gestured to the computer. "I'm not an expert, but I can try searching for nearby short-term rentals."

"I found two possible places, but they are really expensive." Charlotte sighed. "My private donor is trying to raise additional funds."

"Will you let me take a look?"

In answer, she turned the computer screen toward him. The first place was a two-story house located in a residential area. The price tag even for a week-long stay was jaw-dropping, but he had more than enough to cover it. He was more worried about keeping a residential home secure. Lots of windows and more than one entrance were problematic.

The second property was more expensive, but it was also bigger and located farther outside of town. It had six bedrooms and sleeping space for fifteen people. Best of all, it had a security system. "This one for sure. I'll pay for a week-long stay and the bus to get us there."

"I can't ask you to do that," Charlotte protested.

"Why not? You take money from donors all the time. Consider this my donation to the cause."

Charlotte frowned.

"He's right, Char, and you know it," Milly said. "Once the police catch this guy, we can use the funds we've been promised to fix the windows."

"Please let me help you," he urged, turning the screen back toward her. "This place has a security system."

"It's so nice and fancy," Charlotte blurted. "It has a heated pool! I don't want these women to get the idea that all of our safe houses will be as nice as this one. And what if one of the kids break something? I mean, this place looks like something a Hollywood movie star would own."

"I'll take care of the extra cost if something happens, but I think you should give your residents more credit. They're not going to think this is how the average person lives. But to stay here for a week might make them more determined to get their life back on track."

"Or make them more frustrated with their lot in life," Charlotte said wearily. Then she threw up her hands. "Okay, fine. One week. But if Detective Grimes hasn't found the dark-haired guy by then, we'll have to return here until my anonymous donor comes up with another safe house."

"Sounds good." He quickly made the arrangements to pay for the luxurious house, then searched for transportation. As he did that, there was another knock at the door. He started to rise, but Charlotte shook her head.

"I received a text, it's the transportation for Jessie and Maria." She hurried out to get the women.

He continued making their travel arrangements.

"You're a good man, Kaleb," Milly said softly. "I'm glad these women have the chance to see what a real man acts like."

"Ah, thanks, but most men don't abuse women and children."

"Unfortunately, the women here have been exposed to those who do. And often by more than one man in their life."

Kaleb shook his head, wishing things were different. He sent up a silent prayer for God to continue watching over those in need, especially women and children in difficult situations, then made the final payment for the charter bus that would be there in three hours.

He only hoped they could get onto the bus and away from there without the dark-haired man seeing them.

———

CHARLOTTE COULDN'T EXPLAIN why she felt guilty over taking Kaleb's money. Normally, she gladly accepted any and all charity. Beggars could not afford to be choosy after all.

Yet this felt different. More personal. Maybe because of the ridiculous attraction she felt toward him.

Her problem, not his. Kaleb may just be one of the nicest guys she'd ever met, but that didn't mean she had to drool over the man. Besides, she hadn't even known him for twenty-four hours. She'd dated Jerry for six months before she agreed to marry him. And it was only then that she'd been on the receiving end of his violent temper.

This wasn't about her, it was about keeping the women and children safe.

She told herself to shake it off, but it wasn't easy. Watching Emma flirt with him had made her want to yank the girl away, shove her into the closest bedroom, and lock the door behind her.

"Charlotte?" Hearing Kaleb's low, husky voice had her spinning around so fast she fell into the mattress he'd propped against the wall.

"What is it?" She hoped he didn't notice how flustered she was.

"The charter bus will be here in three hours. I need you to tell the women to get ready to move. And we need to pack up the food in the kitchen too."

"After lunch," Milly said from the kitchen. "The spaghetti is ready."

"Three hours is plenty of time," she assured Kaleb. "These women usually don't have much when they come here. That's the reason I keep a large box of spare clothing and small toiletries in the spare room."

"I'll grab that box and any others you have ready to go," Kaleb offered.

"After lunch," she said. "Milly will be upset if you don't eat."

"I'll wait until after everyone else has eaten," Kaleb insisted. Without waiting for her to respond, he turned and went through the living room to the spare bedroom.

"That's a true gentleman for you," Milly said as she dished out plates of spaghetti for their residents.

Charlotte could tell Milly was enamored of Kaleb, which was fine, but they shouldn't become dependent on him. It wasn't like they'd have their own personal body-guard indefinitely. Once they were moved to their new safe house, she figured he'd hit the road, continuing his search for Ava Rampart.

In the short time it took the women and children to eat, Kaleb replaced the mattress on her bed and stacked several boxes near the door. Sierra followed him as he moved from room to room. The man and dog were clearly a team, and if she didn't have women and children dependent on her, she'd consider getting a dog of her own. She pushed that thought aside as being completely impractical under these circumstances.

As their residents made their way to their respective rooms to pack their things, Kaleb and Sierra joined her and Milly in the kitchen.

"Ladies first," he said, gesturing to the stove.

"There's plenty of food," Milly huffed, clearly annoyed at the inference that she hadn't cooked enough to feed an army. "Sit down, young man, and don't give me any lip."

"Yes, ma'am." Kaleb instantly dropped into the closest chair. Sierra stretched out on the floor beside him.

Charlotte smiled. It was funny to watch Kaleb bow down to Milly as if he was following orders from a senior officer. But once they all had their plates of food, Kaleb cleared his throat.

"I'd like to say grace."

Milly lifted her brow, glanced at Charlotte, then said, "I'd like that."

"Dear Lord, we ask You to bless this food, we thank You for keeping us safe in Your care and ask that You continue to protect us from those who seek us harm. Amen."

"Amen," Milly echoed.

"Amen," Charlotte added when they both looked at her expectantly. She wasn't accustomed to praying in general, but it didn't feel as awkward as she'd anticipated.

Yet she didn't really believe God was the reason they'd remained safe throughout these attacks. She depended on herself and most recently now on Kaleb's expertise.

"This is delicious, Milly," Kaleb said after taking a big bite. "Can't remember the last time I had homemade spaghetti."

"Thank you, Kaleb." Milly beamed at his praise. "I'm grateful God sent you here to help us. Feeding you is the least I can do."

Charlotte was unreasonably annoyed with the mutual fan club going on here. "Kaleb, do you have any other leads on where to find Ava? I'm sure you're chomping at the bit to get back on her trail soon."

"I don't have another lead on Ava," Kaleb admitted. Then he eyed her curiously. "Charlotte, I'm not going anywhere until I know you and the others are safe."

"And if they don't find and arrest him?" She waved her fork. "You can't uproot your life for us."

"I'm pretty sure I can do whatever I like," Kaleb pointed out dryly. "I'm not in the navy any longer."

She flushed. "That wasn't what I meant. Your kindness is appreciated, Kaleb, but we know this is temporary. If you did get a new lead on Ava's location, you'd continue your search, wouldn't you?"

He paused, then slowly nodded. "Maybe. If Nico or one of our other teammates couldn't get there to follow up first."

"Exactly." She caught Milly's frown and knew she'd disappointed the woman she loved like a mother. But it was important to her, and really to all their residents, to understand that having Kaleb here protecting them was not a permanent solution.

"The bus will be here at three o'clock?" Milly asked, changing the subject. "I hope I'm ready."

"I'll help you get everything packed, don't worry," Kaleb assured her. "I don't want to take too long getting everything stored on the bus. Better we get in and out of here as quickly as possible."

Charlotte knew he was just as concerned as she was about the gunman potentially getting a glimpse of the bus parked outside. It would be awful if they went through all of this just to have the dark-haired guy follow the bus to their new location.

"We'll be ready to go," she said firmly. "The women know what to do."

Even as she spoke, a few of the women brought their suitcases out from their respective rooms to the hallway, stacking them neatly beside the boxes Kaleb had placed there.

Kaleb ate his meal in record time, then stood and carried his plate to the sink. "I'm assuming I can use the other empty box in the spare room, right? I'll start packing while you finish."

"That's fine." Was the man always like this? Jumping into chores with enthusiasm? Charlotte knew her lack of sleep was likely making her crabby, so she tried to smile at Milly. "He's not one to sit around doing nothing, that's for sure."

"You could do worse than a man like that, Charlotte," Milly said in a scolding tone. "You should be nicer to him. No need to be all prickly."

"I'm not." She glanced over her shoulder to make sure Kaleb wasn't within hearing distance. "Come on, Milly. A man like Kaleb Tyson could have any woman on the planet. There's no reason to think he'd be interested in someone like me. Besides, I don't have the time or energy to become involved in a relationship. I'm too busy sheltering the women and children who need me."

"You deserve to have a life of your own, Charlotte." Milly finished her lunch and hustled over to begin doing the dishes. "And if you ask me, burying yourself here is just a handy excuse to avoid being hurt again."

She was about to argue when Kaleb returned to the kitchen carrying a large box. He set it on the kitchen table. "Do you think the food will fit in here?"

"We'll make it fit." She quickly finished her spaghetti and cleared what was left on the table.

For the next hour, they worked together gathering all the food and staples they'd amassed over the year they'd been there. It didn't take long, but Charlotte still felt depressed at the need to move at all. She liked their current location since the building was closer to the areas that used their services the most.

Abuse victims crossed all lines, race, gender, ethnicity, and economic status. But over the years, she'd noticed the lower income abuse victims tended to be the ones who needed a safe house in the middle of the night.

Those with more money could usually escape to friends or family. If they chose to do so at all.

"Hey, hopefully this is just temporary," Kaleb said, apparently reading her expression. "I have an idea on how to find this guy. Trust me, okay?"

"I do." The words left her lips without her realizing what she was saying. Trust wasn't something she gave freely, especially not to a man she barely knew.

Yet her instincts told her Kaleb was different. Not just because he believed in God and prayed before meals but because he'd gone out of his way to protect them. Sitting outside in the cold all night long? There wasn't a man she knew who would volunteer to do something like that.

He might really be, as Milly had said, one of the good ones.

Thanks to Kaleb's help, they were packed and ready to go well before the three o'clock time frame.

The bus was sleek, black in color, and had tinted windows. Nothing like the school bus she'd used the last time they'd moved. Frankly, she didn't even want to know how much Kaleb had paid for it. The women filed out of the safe house and onto the bus without complaint while Kaleb stored all the boxes and suitcases in the cargo section.

To Charlotte's surprise, they were ready to leave in less than ten minutes. Kaleb disappeared inside, left a light on, then returned, locking the door of the safe house behind him. After climbing onto the bus with Sierra at his heels, he handed her the key.

"Let's go," he told the driver.

The driver nodded and closed the doors. The bus slowly rumbled forward, moving away from the safe house.

Seeing movement along the side of the building across the street, she grabbed Kaleb's muscled arm. "Do you see that man standing by the building? He's wearing a knit hat, so I can't see the color of his hair."

"Stop the bus," he ordered.

The confused driver hit the brake, hard. "What's wrong?"

"Let me out." Kaleb glanced at him impatiently. "Hurry!"

"Wait," Charlotte protested.

"I'll find you later, now go! Hurry!" Kaleb shot over his shoulder as he jumped off the bus. Sierra followed.

"Please go," Charlotte told the driver. He closed the door, put the bus in gear, and pulled back into the street.

She watched as man and dog raced across the street in the direction of the building where she'd seen the man hiding in the shadows.

And for the first time in her life, she prayed for God to protect Kaleb and Sierra from harm.

# CHAPTER FIVE

Kaleb and Sierra ran around the back of the bus toward the location where Charlotte had seen the guy. He'd only gotten a quick glimpse, but the image of a man slinking away while hovering against the side of the building was enough to make him check it out.

No way was he going to let this guy, or anyone else, follow the women and children to the safe house.

Sweeping his gaze over the length of the building, his stomach dropped when he realized the guy was gone. Still, he continued running, ignoring the pain in his bum knee. When he reached the corner, he paused to look both ways.

There! A man dressed in black with a dark knit cap pulled over his head was running several yards up ahead to the right. Dodging pedestrians, he and Sierra went after him.

The man in black disappeared again, forcing Kaleb to put on another burst of speed. No doubt the guy knew the city streets far better than he did. Plus, Kaleb needed to make sure Sierra didn't get hit by a car. The dog wasn't on leash, but thankfully, he'd trained her to stay beside him as they ran.

When he reached the next intersection, he instinctively turned right, knowing the guy wouldn't risk crossing the street. The traffic wasn't horrible, but there were enough cars to slow him down.

There was no sign of the guy up ahead. Had he turned down a side street? Kaleb pressed forward, refusing to give up. He wanted, *needed* to get this guy.

If he was in fact the same dark-haired guy who'd shot the safe house twice in less than twenty-four hours.

He slowed his pace, looking from side to side to figure out where the lurker had gone. Kaleb frowned when he spied a black knit hat on the ground.

Kneeling beside it, he debated the likelihood that it belonged to the lurker. Considering it was wintertime, it could belong to anyone.

But he didn't think so. He fished in his pocket for a baggie—he always carried several eco-friendly bags to clean up after Sierra—and used it to pick up the hat. After pocketing the bag, he continued, hoping to find the man it belonged to.

Fifteen minutes later, Kaleb knew it was futile. The guy must have gotten away, going down one of the side streets, an alley, maybe even ducking into one of the businesses and escaping out the back.

"Okay, girl. Time to take a break." Kaleb leaned against the side of a café, rubbing his right knee. Sierra sat beside him, and he had to smile at how she didn't look the least bit tired after their romp.

The dog was in much better shape than a busted-up former Navy SEAL, that was for sure.

Kaleb dug for his phone and called Detective Grimes. The guy answered quickly. "Tyson? Something wrong?"

"I chased after a guy lurking outside the safe house. He was wearing a black knit cap, and I found one lying on the street. I'm hoping you can check it for DNA."

Grimes didn't say anything for a long moment. "Did you see him drop it?"

"No. But the guy I chased was wearing one, so it's more than likely his."

"The law doesn't work that way," Grimes said in a weary tone. "I can't use that hat for evidence. Especially when the guy you chased hadn't done anything wrong."

Kaleb stared up at the sky for a moment before sighing. "I was afraid you'd say that."

"Listen, why don't you let me handle the investigation? If you want to hang around to keep the women and children safe, that's fine. But I'll do the rest."

Kaleb decided against pointing out that so far the detective hadn't come up with squat. "Okay, fine, but I'm going to keep this hat with me. If we get a suspect in custody, you might be able to use it then."

"Doubtful. Anything else?" There was a note of impatience in his tone.

"No. That's it." Kaleb disconnected from the call. He wasn't a cop, didn't have a degree in criminal justice, but he certainly understood there were formal police procedures.

Personally, he liked it better when he was a SEAL following orders. The ops he and the rest of the team had taken on were approved at the highest level of the government, all the way up to the president himself. No need to follow pesky rules.

Adjusting to civilian life hadn't been easy. Sierra had helped him on an emotional level, but now that he was trying to find Ava and keep Charlotte and the others safe, he didn't appreciate the constraints he was forced to work within.

"Come on, girl." He pushed away from the building. "We need to meet up with Charlotte and the others at the safe house."

Sierra wagged her tail in agreement.

Kaleb used his phone to find his current location. He'd left an overnight bag, along with some of Sierra's supplies, in his motel room. He realized the motel wasn't that far and decided to walk. From there, he'd use a rideshare to get to the new safe house.

After returning to the motel, he packed his stuff and checked out. He called for a rideshare, going through several attempts since finding one that allowed dogs wasn't easy, then gave the driver a location that was a full mile from his final destination.

Maybe it was overly paranoid, but he figured the fewer people having the address, the better. He purposefully hadn't given their new location to Detective Grimes.

The only bright side of this little detour was that chasing the lurker had likely prevented him from following the bus. That alone made this delay well worth it.

Sierra stretched out on the seat beside him, resting her head in his lap, her dark eyes closed. He stroked her silky black fur, wishing he could fall asleep as easily. The adrenaline crash after chasing the lurker and the measly three hours of sleep were starting to catch up to him. He yawned and rested his head against the window.

"Buddy? We're here."

Kaleb blinked and straightened. Somehow, he'd managed a thirty-minute nap. "Thanks." He added a tip to the driver's fee and then slid out of the vehicle. Slinging his gear over his shoulder, he set out walking.

The neighborhood was several steps—more likely a twenty-story elevator ride—above what they'd left behind. Walking didn't hurt his knee as much as running, enabling him to keep a brisk pace. He was anxious to get to the safe house. The idea of leaving Charlotte, Milly, and the others there alone bothered him.

To his surprise, the black charter bus was still in the driveway when he arrived. The rideshare must have made better time. He hurried forward, wincing when he saw Charlotte struggling to remove one of the boxes from the cargo hold.

"I'll get that," he protested.

"Kaleb? You're here!" His heart soared when she smiled, her eyes bright with joy. "How did you get here so quickly?"

"No clue." He gently nudged her aside to grab the box. "Lead the way."

"Look at this kitchen," Milly gushed as they went inside. "I've never cooked a meal in something so fancy!"

"The whole place is fancy," Emma said, her gaze lingering on him as he set the box inside. "And we owe Kaleb a debt of gratitude for being here."

"We do," Charlotte agreed. "Emma, will you please help Milly unpack the food?"

"Sure." He could feel Emma watching him for a long moment before she joined Milly. Kaleb inwardly sighed, wishing Emma would worry about her future after leaving the safe house rather than staring at him.

He turned his attention to Charlotte. "I'll unload the rest of the boxes, and you can tell me where you want them."

"Thanks." Charlotte followed him outside. "I take it you didn't catch him?"

"No." He hefted another box from the cargo area. "I chased him for several minutes, but he got away. I did find a knit hat on the ground, though, that may have belonged to him."

Her eyes lit up. "Does that mean we can trace his DNA?"

"Grimes won't do that because I didn't see him drop the hat." Charlotte opened the door for him. "But I kept the hat anyway."

"That box goes upstairs," she said. "It has my things and Milly's inside. The women are discussing the rest of the sleeping arrangements, but Milly and I have called dibs on the master suite."

"Well deserved," Kaleb said, carrying the box up the sweeping staircase. She led the way, and he set the box on the floor at the foot of the bed. "It's nice."

She waved a hand. "This is the most extravagant place I've ever stayed. It feels like a minivacation."

"I'm glad." He grinned. "You should enjoy the pool while you can."

She blushed and turned away. "Come on, there's more work to be done. Oh, and if you want one of the bedrooms, let me know. I can make the others double up if needed."

"That's not necessary, I'd prefer to sleep on the living room sofa." He followed her downstairs, trying not to imagine the gun-toting pixie wearing a swimsuit the same color as her aquamarine eyes, but it wasn't easy.

He was a man after all.

Less than an hour later, they had everything put away. He tipped the bus driver and reminded him that confidentiality was key. "Don't tell anyone about where these women are, understand?"

The guy nodded, his expression grim. "Sad situation all around," he said. "I don't understand it."

"Me either. But I appreciate your help today." Kaleb stepped back and watched as he drove away.

A sense of excitement and anticipation was in the air. The women and children who had mostly kept to themselves were chattering brightly about their new surroundings. The kids, of course, wanted to swim, and he was happy that Charlotte encouraged it.

"Keep an eye on them, though," she warned. "The pool is heated, but the air is still cool. And we don't want any tragic accidents here. I'm not sure how well these kids know how to swim."

"We will," the women assured her.

"I plan to join them," another said with a laugh. "I don't care how cold the air is, I'm going to enjoy every moment."

Kaleb moved closer to Charlotte as they headed upstairs. "I can't remember hearing them laugh before."

"That's because they didn't have anything to laugh about." Charlotte shrugged and smiled. "I wasn't keen on the idea of coming here, but it seems like a break from their usual world will be a nice change. As long as they don't get used to living in the lap of luxury."

"I think they understand this is temporary," Kaleb assured her. "Have you figured out how to use the security system?"

"The property owner left instructions." She touched his arm, drawing him to the gleaming marble counter to a small spiral notebook. "The key code to get into the house is different from the security system, which means we have two codes to memorize. The security system is an older model not connected to the Wi-Fi. According to the notes left by the owner, it was installed back when the house was built. The instructions were basic enough."

He read through the directions, keenly aware of Charlotte standing beside him. Maybe the female residents weren't the only ones who needed to remember this was a temporary arrangement. He liked spending time with Charlotte Cambridge far too much.

"I—uh, better go outside." He forced himself to take a step back, almost tripping over Sierra standing behind him. "I need to walk the property to understand the various strengths and weaknesses of the place."

"Of course." Charlotte nodded toward the kitchen. "Milly said to plan on dinner at six."

"Thanks." He crossed over to the front door, took a moment to disarm the alarm, then headed outside. "Come, Sierra."

The dog eagerly followed. He engaged the alarm system and began to explore the various doorways and lower-level windows. The alarm was helpful, but that alone wouldn't keep them safe.

No, this guy had already proven his weapon of choice was a gun. The assailant could shoot and kill someone through one of the many windows easily enough. Sure, the alarm would sound, but it would go off too late.

He purposefully stayed outside until it was close to dinnertime, enjoying the laughter as the kids swam in the pool. He cleaned up after Sierra, thinking again about the knit hat he'd tucked into his pocket. He knew Bravo, Mason's dog, was a scent tracker. He'd done some work with Sierra but hadn't tested her on many individual scents.

Yet, it couldn't hurt to try. Dogs were smart, more so than most pet owners gave them credit for. He spent a few extra minutes outside, offering Sierra the knit cap to smell. "Bad Man," he said in a harsh tone. "Bad Man."

He wasn't sure Sierra really understood, but as she walked beside him, lifting her nose to the air, he felt certain she would recognize the scent if she experienced it again.

As he returned to head back inside, he told himself they were as well protected as they could be under the circumstances.

He silently prayed it would be enough.

---

THE VACATION-LIKE ATMOSPHERE in their plush accommodations had an incredible effect on the residents. The women were getting along like old friends, when in reality they barely knew each other, and the kids were jumping up and down with excitement. Charlotte had never seen a transformation like this before and wished it was something they could fit into their budget on an ongoing basis.

About as likely as flying pink elephants dropping from the sky, but hey, it was nice to dream.

The numerous large windows were a little nerve-racking. Charlotte found herself glancing at them frequently, half expecting to see a man standing outside with a gun. Twice she'd glimpsed Kaleb and Sierra moving about outside. Humbling, really, the way he took their safety so seriously.

She owed him more than she could ever repay. Not just for protecting them the past twenty-four hours but for financing and arranging this place for them to use. None of this would be possible if not for his kind generosity.

Even more amazing was that he didn't want anything in return.

"Oh, Kaleb, you're just in time for dinner," Emma gushed.

"I didn't have a lot of time, so we're just having grilled cheese sandwiches and soup," Milly said in an apologetic tone. "But I'm going to make a nice pot roast for tomorrow."

"Both options sound great," Kaleb assured her. Charlotte was impressed he didn't encourage Emma's behavior. "I'll wash up a bit, and I need to feed Sierra too."

"I'll help!" Emma said, jumping up from her seat.

"No, Sierra only eats food I give her." Kaleb's tone was mild, but his gaze was serious. "I'll be ready shortly."

Emma looked upset as she sat down, and despite being somewhat annoyed by the girl's behavior, Charlotte hated seeing her like that. "He's trained Sierra to only eat food he offers her to prevent anyone from poisoning her. I've read that's a very common practice with police K9 dogs too."

"That's awful," Jodie spoke up. "No one should poison a dog."

"There's a lot of things that shouldn't happen," Kim muttered under her breath. "We all know that more than anyone."

A grim silence fell for a long moment, Kim's statement a sobering reminder of why they were together in the first place.

When Kaleb joined them, he took a seat beside Charlotte. "I'd like to say grace."

"Go ahead," Milly encouraged, folding her hands and bowing her head.

The residents looked at each other questioningly, then followed suit. Charlotte did too.

"Dear Lord, we thank You for guiding us to safety

today. We ask You to bless this food, bless our temporary living arrangements, and to continue protecting everyone seated here this evening. Amen."

"Amen," Milly echoed.

There was a spattering response of amens from the rest of the group before they dug in to their food. Charlotte could tell Kaleb's prayer had been an oddity for the women and children seated at the table.

Including her.

She didn't know any men who prayed the way Kaleb did. Was his faith related to his time in the service as a Navy SEAL? Being in constant danger, living under extreme conditions couldn't have been easy.

Kaleb's inner strength was admirable. Then again, she found just about everything about him admirable.

"This is delicious, Milly," Kaleb said with a smile at the older woman. "You're a great cook."

"Why thank you, Kaleb." Milly blushed like a schoolgirl beneath his praise. "I made extra sandwiches, so please help yourself."

"Can we swim again after dinner?" Tommy asked. He was the oldest of the three kids and had been unnaturally silent until today.

"Maybe tomorrow," Willow said. She rested her hand on her son's head. "It's much colder outside now. We need to wait until the sun comes out, okay? That will be something fun to look forward to."

Tommy looked disappointed but then nodded. "Can I play the soccer video game, then?"

"Yes, but only until bedtime. And remember the rule, every argument you make about not wanting to go to bed means you lose thirty minutes of playing time."

Tommy rolled his eyes. "I know, I know."

Kaleb gazed over at Tommy with a longing that made her think he wished he had a child of his own.

She understood how he felt. Years ago, she'd anticipated getting married, having children, and living happily ever after. Yeah, that so hadn't happened. She told herself that wishing for something she couldn't have was ridiculous. Better to stay focused on what was important. Finding the identity of the dark-haired man and having him arrested.

Then continuing her work of keeping abused women and children safe from harm.

When dinner was finished, Kim and Willow went into the kitchen to start cleaning up. Charlotte was happy to see they'd done their assigned duty without being told.

"Charlotte? Do you have a minute?" Kaleb asked.

"Sure." She followed him into the main living space. Then frowned when she saw the sofa. "You can't sleep there, it's too short. You'll never be comfortable on that thing."

"I'll be fine." He waved off her concern. "But I wanted to mention something about the swimming pool."

She frowned. "Like what?"

"The security system doesn't cover the patio and pool area, it's only wired to the house." His gaze was troubled. "The patio doors are connected to the system, so that's good, but being outside is a problem. I don't want to disappoint the kids, but they shouldn't be out there without me watching over them."

Charlotte nodded slowly. She understood his concern, and it was something she should have thought about earlier. "I'll discuss that with the women tomorrow. As Willow said, it's too cold to swim at night anyway. Even in a heated pool. It would be nice, though, to carve out an hour of swim time in the middle of the day."

"I'm sure we can make that work." He stared into her eyes for a moment as if there was more he wanted to say, then glanced away.

"I'd feel better if you'd let me ask one of the others to sleep on the sofa," she said.

"No need, besides, I like that you're all upstairs on the second floor. Better for me to be down here in case someone does try to come in." He moved toward the too-short sofa. "Once everyone goes upstairs, Sierra and I will do another walk around the perimeter."

"Okay, thanks." She forced herself to let it go, no doubt Kaleb had likely slept in worse spots than a cramped sofa.

Charlotte's phone rang, and she quickly answered when she recognized her donor's name. "Hi, Abby."

"I'm sorry I couldn't get back to you sooner, but I did get some additional funding," Abby informed her. "Do you need help moving yet tonight?"

Casting her gaze around the magnificent house, she couldn't help but grin. "Nope, I had another donor arrange new digs. However, this is only temporary, we only have a week. If this guy isn't caught by then, I'll need a new, longer-term location."

"Is the donor anyone I know?" Abby asked.

"I don't think so." For some reason, she didn't want to let Abby know her donor was a man. "But thanks for everything you've done. I am very grateful, and the women and children here are too."

"You're welcome. I wish . . ." Abby's voice trailed off. Charlotte knew the older woman was thinking about how she hadn't escaped her abusive relationship before her husband had died of cancer. "Whatever. It doesn't matter. I guess God was watching over me. This way I get to use

Frank's money for something good. Something he'd hate," she added with a wry chuckle.

"You're making a huge difference in the lives of these women and children, Abby," Charlotte reminded her. "That's what's most important."

"I know. Take care, Char. Call me with an update in a few days, okay?"

"I will, thanks again." She disconnected from the call and headed upstairs. The events of the day must have worn on everyone because by eight thirty, the women and their respective children were settled in their respective rooms.

Charlotte tried to sleep. She was physically and emotionally exhausted, but sharing the king bed with Milly meant listening to the older woman's soft snoring. After an hour, she slid out of bed and padded downstairs.

Milly strongly believed in the power of drinking Sleepy-time tea. Charlotte had tried it several times, with varying degrees of success. When she reached the bottom of the stairs, she paused, straining to listen. The last thing she wanted to do was to wake Kaleb. The man had barely gotten any sleep that morning before the gunfire had ruined their day.

When she didn't hear anything, she tiptoed across the tile floor to the kitchen. She hesitated, thinking it might be better to simply turn around to go back to bed. Using the microwave to heat water might be enough to wake him up.

"Can't sleep?"

Kaleb's voice startled her so badly she jumped around and stubbed her big toe on the edge of the lower cabinet. She winced and leaned down to rub her injured foot. "You scared me! Why don't you wear a bell?"

"A bell?" His eyebrows hiked up, and he grinned. "Not a bad idea, especially since I know you're packing heat."

She rolled her eyes at his teasing. "Not in my pajamas," she retorted. "I thought you were asleep."

"The sofa is too short." When she opened her mouth to argue, his grin widened. "Just kidding. Honestly, I dozed for a while but woke when I heard you come down. The third stair from the bottom creaks a bit."

"I hadn't noticed. Sorry, I didn't mean to wake you." She lowered her foot and turned to search for the tea. The kitchen cabinets were higher than what she was used to, and of course, Milly had put the coffee and tea on the higher of the two shelves.

She lifted up on her tippy toes to get it, but then Kaleb was there reaching over her shoulder. He was so close and smelled so good.

"Uh, thanks." Was that breathless voice really hers? She sounded like a Marilyn Monroe wannabe.

She tried to move to the side but hit her injured big toe again. Swallowing the urge to swear, something she didn't allow any of the residents to do, she made another grab at her foot.

"Did I hurt you?" Kaleb's strong hands cupped her shoulders. "I'm so sorry."

"It's fine." She looked up at him at the same moment he lowered his head toward her.

The next second, he was kissing her, cradling her against his chest as he devoured her mouth in a heated embrace she prayed would never stop.

# CHAPTER SIX

His adorable pixie tasted like peppermint. He decided peppermint was his new favorite flavor. At some level, Kaleb knew he was crossing the line, but he couldn't seem to make himself care.

This was what he'd wanted the first moment he'd seen her standing in the doorway holding a gun trained at the center of his chest. He'd thought about kissing her, but his imagination hadn't done her justice. She tasted incredible.

He'd never wanted a woman more.

When Sierra nudged him, he wanted to push the dog away, but Charlotte broke off from the kiss. Her breathing erratic, much like his own.

"Wow," he murmured, trailing the tip of his finger down her silky cheek. "That was amazing."

"I—uh—need to . . ." Her voice trailed off, and he couldn't help but grin at her inability to formulate a coherent sentence.

"Drink your Sleepytime tea?" He badly wanted to kiss her again but figured he shouldn't press his luck. For one thing, he didn't want to scare her. He shouldn't have pounced like a drowning man gasping for air.

But the most important reason was that he refused to take advantage of the situation. They were only here together because some abuser was seeking revenge.

"Yes." She pulled out of his embrace and stared blankly for a moment at the small box of tea sitting on the counter. Then she picked it up, took out a tea bag, and grabbed a mug from the cupboard. The way she avoided his gaze as she went through the process of warming up the water in the microwave made him pause.

Maybe he had scared her or did something to bring bad memories floating to the surface. *Idiot*, he silently rebuked. *Couldn't you have handled that with more gentleness?*

"Charlotte. Do I need to apologize? I didn't mean to frighten you."

"No!" She spun away from the microwave to face him. "You didn't. It's just—" She waved a hand. "I don't know. I wasn't expecting that."

"The kiss? Or the impact of it?"

Finally, the corner of her mouth tipped up in a wry smile. "Both."

"Okay, I can work with that." The moment he said the words, she shook her head and took a step back.

"No, Kaleb. We both know this isn't going anywhere. I've dedicated my life to protecting women and children, providing them a safe place to live. At this point, I'm not interested in anything else."

"I see." He didn't really understand at all, but now that he was thinking more clearly, he knew she might be right. He didn't particularly care for Los Angeles and hadn't planned to stay other than to find Ava. Still, a stab of disappointment hit hard. "Thanks for letting me know."

She narrowed her gaze, planting her hands on her hips in a defiant stance. "Come on, Kaleb. You don't have to act like you were looking for a relationship. You could have any woman you wanted, why pick one that has more baggage than a jumbo jet?"

"Everyone has a past, Charlotte. A history." He hated that she felt unlovable. Or maybe unworthy of being cared for. "You know my past, I was married once, when I was young and foolish. I know your life must not have been all sunshine and roses either. Maybe one day you'll be willing to share what you endured, but no pressure. You should know that you're an attractive woman, Charlotte. And any man would count his blessings to have you in his life."

Her eyes widened, and she opened her mouth, then closed it again as if she had no clue what to say.

The microwave dinged, and she turned away to make her tea.

Sierra nudged him again, harder this time. He sighed and glanced down at her. "Okay, okay. We'll go outside."

Cradling the mug in her hands, Charlotte leaned against the counter. He wanted to stay, to see if she might reveal more about her past, but she remained silent.

He offered her a smile. "Enjoy your tea. I'll be back soon. Come, Sierra." He led the dog to the front door, deactivated the alarm to take her out, then keyed the code in to activate it again.

Since they were outside, he walked the perimeter of the property. He estimated the house sat on a half an acre of land, unusually large for the Los Angeles suburbs. Then again, it appeared the homeowners had plenty of money.

He liked that the house wasn't sitting on top of a neighbor's house. Even better, he was relieved to find everything was fine. No sign that an intruder had been there.

As much as he was glad they'd gotten away from the previous safe house without being followed, he wished the guy hadn't seen the bus at all. Kaleb had given up his original plan to sit at the safe house, hoping the gunman would return. After the guy had basically watched them get onto the bus, Kaleb had known that trying to trap the guy into coming inside the safe house would be a useless endeavor. The guy would be stupid to return to their previous location, knowing full well it was empty.

He desperately needed a new plan. Unfortunately, without a name, or even a clear photograph of the guy, he couldn't come up with one.

Lifting his gaze to the sky, he silently prayed. *Please, Lord, grant me the wisdom and strength to find this evil man!*

As always, Kaleb felt a sense of calm after praying. When he'd finished the perimeter check, he led Sierra back inside.

He was disappointed, though, to find Charlotte had gone back upstairs, leaving her empty tea mug on the counter. He hoped she'd finally fall asleep, getting the rest she needed.

Something he needed to do as well.

Sierra followed him to the living room. The sofa was too short, but he bent his knees up to his chest and slept on his side. It wasn't the most comfortable position, his bum knee didn't love it, but he'd slept in worse conditions.

One minute he was listening to Sierra's breathing, the next he was flailing in the water, trying to survive after an underwater bomb exploded meters from their SEAL team.

*Can't breathe! Can't breathe!* His world was upside down, he couldn't figure out which way to go to reach the surface. His BUD/S training came back to him, but trying to see the direction the bubbles were rising was much harder when the entire ocean was rolling in turmoil.

The pressure in his chest increased to an intolerable level. His head throbbed painfully. Just when he thought he might die, his head broke through the surface. He gasped seconds before the turbulent water sucked him down again.

*No!*

Kaleb woke with a start, his body sticky with sweat. He was breathing heavily, as if he truly was drowning again. Sierra licked his face. He reached out a hand to stroke her, realizing the dog had once again woken him from the horrific nightmare. His head still hurt, but not with as much force as he'd experienced in the past. A sign he was getting slightly better? Maybe.

"Kaleb? Are you okay?"

He winced, turning to see Charlotte standing at the end of the sofa. "Yes, fine." His voice sounded rough, as if he really had swallowed half the ocean. "Sorry I woke you."

"You didn't, I normally get up early." Her eyes were full of concern.

He belatedly realized dawn was peeking over the horizon. Somehow, he'd managed to get a solid seven hours of sleep. Until the nightmare had struck again. "Ah, that's great. I hope you slept well?"

She nodded. "The Sleepytime tea worked. Maybe you should have tried some."

He scrubbed his hands over his face. "No need, I slept fine." And he had, until the past came back to haunt him.

Charlotte didn't look convinced, but she didn't press for more. "I usually enjoy a cup of coffee before everyone else wakes up. Care to join me?"

"I'd love to, but I need to take Sierra out first."

"That's okay, by the time you return, the coffee will be ready." She headed into the kitchen.

He took a moment to rub Sierra, kissing her nose. "Thanks, girl. You're a lifesaver."

Sierra wagged her tail and licked his chin.

After he finished cleaning up after his best friend, he brought Sierra back inside and headed into the kitchen. He needed a shower, but he wasn't about to give up even one minute of alone time with Charlotte.

"Black, right?" She glanced at him, holding up the pot.

"Yes, please."

Charlotte handed him a mug of coffee, then doctored hers with cream and sugar before joining him at the breakfast bar. "I only drink it for the caffeine," she joked.

He chuckled. "Trust me, that is not unusual. Coffee is a staple in the navy, and the other branches of the military too, I'm sure."

"I can imagine," she agreed. "I'm sorry you suffered a nightmare."

He shrugged and sipped from his mug. "I don't have them as often as I used to." He looked down at Sierra, lying at his feet. "Sierra has been a huge help. She keeps me grounded and always wakes me up before I—" He caught himself before blurting the word *die*.

"Oh, Kaleb." Charlotte reached out to cover his hand with hers. "That sounds awful."

It wasn't fun, but he really didn't care to dwell on it. "I'm alive, and that's what matters." He took another sip of his coffee. "What's the plan for today?"

"You know the kids will want to swim at least for an hour or so. Otherwise, no big plans." She frowned. "I feel like we should be doing something, though, to figure out who this guy is."

"I understand. I'll call Detective Grimes, see if he has any updates." He thought about the knit hat. "I can try heading back to the safe house, see if Sierra can track the guy's scent."

Charlotte's eyes widened. "She can do that?"

"I'm not sure, but it can't hurt to try." He wouldn't lie to her. "I've only just started doing some scent training with her. She's a smart dog, but I don't think she's at the level of a police or military K9 yet, either, so don't get your hopes up."

"Right now, doing anything is better than sitting here and worrying." Charlotte braced her elbows on the table. "I've been thinking maybe I should go back to the safe house, make it look as if we've returned."

"No!" He tried to dial back his panic. "There's no need. Let me see what Sierra can do first. And we'll follow up with Grimes too. After all, he's the one who should be out searching for this guy."

"I'm sure he's doing his best."

Kaleb knew she was right, but Grimes's best wasn't good enough. But before he could say anything more, Milly entered the room.

"Char, you're up early today." The sweet housekeeper beamed at him. "You too, Kaleb."

"Military habits," he said with a grin. "I'm happy to see you too, Ms. Milly. I believe your being here is an indication that breakfast is right around the corner."

Milly giggled. "Of course, I'm planning to make French toast this morning. It's a favorite with the kiddos."

"Sounds good to me." Kaleb couldn't remember the last time he'd had French toast. Maybe as a kid growing up, but now that his parents were gone, both dying of different forms of cancer—breast cancer for his mom and colon cancer for his dad—he hadn't thought about those Sunday breakfasts in years. The navy tended to stick with the basics, powdered eggs and toast, maybe bacon or sausage on a rare occasion. His mouth watered with anticipation. "Thanks."

Soon the rest of the residents emerged from their rooms.

Kaleb decided to wait until later, after he'd taken the kids outside to swim, before heading back to the original safe house. Yesterday, when he'd watched the kids play while the women chatted amongst themselves, he had to admit that Charlotte's mission was an honorable one.

Not that her doing this meant she couldn't have a meaningful relationship of her own, but he appreciated what she'd accomplished here. To see these abuse survivors talking, smiling, and even sometimes laughing was heartwarming.

God had clearly brought him to Los Angeles and Charlotte's safe house to protect them. He was more than willing to accept the challenge.

The morning went by fast, and once they'd finished with lunch, the kids were begging and pleading to swim. The sun had warmed the temperatures to seventy-five, which wasn't hot, but it wasn't freezing either.

The kids and several of the women enjoyed the pool. Emma flirted with him, but he pretended not to notice. He and Sierra walked around the pool like sentinels on duty.

Charlotte didn't swim, which was a disappointment. He told himself to be thankful for small favors. It was difficult enough to forget the impact of her peppermint kiss, and seeing her in a swimsuit would not help.

The kids were shivering by two o'clock in the afternoon. Their mothers forced them to come out of the water to dry off. Once everyone was inside, he activated the alarm and went to find Charlotte.

"Sierra and I are heading out," he informed her. "I need you to keep everyone inside with the alarm system activated."

"I will."

His phone rang. Seeing Detective Grimes's name on the screen, he quickly answered, putting the call on speaker so she could hear. "Hello?"

"Tyson? I have another photo array I'd like to show Ms. Cambridge."

He locked gazes with Charlotte. "Yes, I'm here, Detective. Kaleb and I can be there in thirty minutes."

"Sounds good. I'll be waiting."

Kaleb disconnected the call and stared at her. "Are you sure about this? Leaving them here alone?"

"Milly can watch over them. It's more important for me to help identify the man responsible."

He nodded. "Okay, it looks like we're both going into the city then." He moved away to call for a rideshare.

Oddly enough, he wasn't disappointed that she'd be going with him. Which only told him he was in trouble.

Deep, deep trouble.

---

THE FEELING of anticipation was out of proportion with the task before her. Charlotte knew she was only going to identify a suspect, there was no reason to be giddy about spending time with Kaleb.

But she was.

She blamed the kiss. The incredible, toe-curling, thought-spiraling, desire-provoking kiss. She'd spent most of the day reminding herself that kissing Kaleb again could not happen. She liked her life the way it was, thank you very much. The last thing she wanted was a relationship fraught with complications.

Besides, when she'd pointed out that things between them couldn't go anywhere, Kaleb had not disagreed. The moment the danger was over, he would leave to continue searching for Ava. Or doing whatever former SEALs did.

While she continued managing a safe house for abused women and children.

"Ready?" Kaleb asked as a blue SUV rolled down the street.

"Of course." The rideshare driver stopped at the end of the driveway. Kaleb held the door open for her, then gestured for Sierra to hop in before he followed.

"Thanks for the ride," Kaleb said as the guy pulled away from the curb.

The driver shrugged. "Just make sure the dog doesn't mess up my car."

"She won't."

Charlotte stroked her hand over Sierra's fur. "She's incredibly well behaved."

"She's a great companion," Kaleb agreed. He leaned closer, lowering his voice. "After we meet with Grimes, we'll head over to the safe house. See if she can pick up the scent from the knit cap I found."

"I'd like that." Truthfully, Charlotte was looking forward to watching Sierra in action. She felt good about the possibility of getting the gunman behind bars. The dark-haired man had to be a former boyfriend or husband of one of the women in the shelter. Personally, she hoped it was Tommy's father, Willow's ex-husband. The guy deserved to be locked up for beating Willow and giving his son a black eye.

Despite the notorious Los Angeles traffic, the trip to the

police station didn't take as long as she'd feared. When they arrived, Kaleb called Grimes to let them know they were there.

"I have Sierra with me, and I'm armed," Kaleb said. "You may want to meet us outside the building."

She assumed the detective agreed because less than two minutes later, he strode out of the police station looking annoyed. "Why would you bring a gun here?"

"Because, like you, I don't go anywhere without it." Kaleb waved an impatient hand. "What does it matter? I have a permit. Now, show us what you have."

Grimes muttered something under his breath and held out the photo array. Charlotte took it from him, staring intently at the photos. She examined one photo at a time, trying to remember the brief glimpses she'd gotten of the dark-haired man.

As she moved from one picture to the next, she grew disheartened. One photo in particular was close, but she honestly didn't think it was the same man.

"See something familiar?" Grimes asked as if reading her indecision.

"Wait, let me look them over too." Kaleb took the photo array from her hand. He scanned them carefully, then glanced at her. "Okay, which one did you think was a possibility?"

"This one." She pointed to the last photo on the card. "I can't be sure, but he's similar to the man I saw."

"There is a resemblance," Kaleb agreed. "But I can't swear it's the same man either."

"If he's a possible suspect, I can bring him in for questioning," Grimes said with a shrug. "Can't hurt to hear what he has to say."

Charlotte frowned. "Do you really think he'll confess to shooting the safe house?"

"No, but I've been doing this a long time, I can often pick up when I'm being lied to." Grimes took the photo array back. "It's worth a try, right?"

"Right. Are there more suspects to track down?" Kaleb asked.

"No." Grimes glanced at her. "Unless you can give me more victim names, this is all I came up with."

She swallowed a stab of disappointment. "I gave you all the names of the women who'd been here the past two months. We can go back further, but it seems odd that this guy would be looking for her after all this time."

"I don't know, I think you should do that anyway," Kaleb said. "It could be that he'd been doing jail time, and if that's the case, you should not underestimate the power of revenge."

He had a good point. "Okay, I'll compile another list and get that to you, Detective." She forced a smile. "Thanks for all your help on this situation."

"Not a problem. I want to find this guy too. I'll keep you updated if I come up with anything more." Grimes began to turn away.

"Wait." Kaleb lightly grasped his arm. "Can you tell us the name of that guy? The one we both thought resembled the man we saw?"

Grimes hesitated. "I shouldn't tell you, we don't know that he's guilty of anything."

"I'm not going to stalk him," Kaleb said. "I'm just curious which of the women he's connected with."

Grimes was silent for so long she doubted he'd admit to anything. Finally, he said, "His name is Thomas Acker, but you didn't hear that from me." Grimes shook off Kaleb's hand and headed inside.

"Thomas Acker!" Charlotte grasped Kaleb's hand at the revelation. "That's Willow's ex-husband. Tommy's father!"

"The kid with a black eye," Kaleb murmured, nodding slowly. "Maybe he is our guy."

"Oh, Kaleb. I wish we could prove that one way or the other. I know Willow and Tommy are scared to death of him."

"Let's head back to the safe house. We know the guy wearing the knit hat was there, so that's a good starting point. We'll see if Sierra picks up his scent."

Charlotte knew pinning their hopes on a partially trained dog wasn't smart, but what choice did they have? The more she thought about the gunman being Thomas Acker, the more convinced she was that he was the stalker.

"Don't, Charlotte," Kaleb said as they began walking. "Neither one of us could say with any degree of certainty that he's the guy."

"I know." She blew out a breath. "You're right. It was close, but not exact. I wouldn't be able to swear to it under oath."

"I couldn't swear to it either. Which is why we need to be careful and keep an open mind. To consider other possible suspects."

Kaleb was right. She glanced at Sierra trotting along between them. "I promise to keep an open mind."

"Technically, Grimes shouldn't have given us the suspect's name," Kaleb said. "I knew I was pushing it, but I didn't expect him to comply."

"Why do you think he did?"

Kaleb smiled. "Honestly? I think he respects the fact that I served our country as a Navy SEAL. I wasn't a cop the way he is, but I did my fair share of tracking down bad guys while fighting for justice. In some ways, the cop mentality is very similar to the military mindset. We both put our lives on the line every day to protect others."

"That makes sense. And I want you to know how much I appreciate how you served our country."

Kaleb nodded but didn't say anything. Remembering the horrible nightmare he'd suffered earlier that morning, she couldn't blame him.

He'd given his life for others. Similar in some respects to what she was trying to do with the women's shelter.

She silently hoped Thomas Acker would be caught doing something illegal. If he wasn't the gunman, she would still rest easier knowing he was behind bars.

When they reached the safe house, Kaleb paused at the corner and pulled out what looked like a poop bag from his pocket. He opened the bag and offered it to Sierra.

"This is Bad Man," he said in a stern voice. "Seek! Seek Bad Man!"

Sierra took a long time sniffing at the knit cap, then wagged her tail when Kaleb pulled a tennis ball from another pocket. He showed it to her, then gave the command again. "Seek!"

Sierra put her nose in the air, then began trotting. She moved from side to side, then went straight over to the side of the building where the man had stood while they were getting everything packed on the bus.

"Good girl! Seek Bad Man!" Kaleb said.

Sierra continued going, following the side of the building. At the next intersection, she turned to the right. Kaleb and Sierra set a quick pace, forcing Charlotte to run to keep up. They dodged pedestrians who eyed them curiously.

"Is this the right way?" she asked breathlessly.

"So far, yeah." Kaleb looked pleased. "Seek!"

Sierra came to a sudden stop, sniffing along the ground for several minutes before sitting down and staring at Kaleb.

"Good girl!" He pulled the ball out of his pocket and tossed it in the air. Sierra jumped up, snapping her jaws around it before the ball could hit the ground.

"What is this place?" Charlotte asked.

"This is the exact spot where I found the knit cap," Kaleb explained. "I need to reward her, then we'll keep going."

Charlotte was impressed with Sierra's ability so far. Was it possible the dog would lead them to the dark-haired guy?

She instinctively turned to prayer, even though she didn't normally do that.

*Please, Lord, help us find him!*

# CHAPTER SEVEN

Sierra was doing better than he'd expected. She seemed to enjoy the game of seeking the bad man, jumping up and down when he rewarded her with the tennis ball. Kaleb hoped and prayed the trail would lead somewhere useful.

After tossing the ball for her, he tucked it away and opened the bag again, offering her the knit cap. As earlier, she readily sniffed it.

"Bad Man," he said in a stern voice. Then he lightened his tone, making sure she understood the name of the game. "Seek! Seek the bad man!"

Sierra went in a circle, ending up back at the spot where Kaleb had found it. He didn't say anything, so she lifted her nose and moved to the right, down a side street.

He tried not to get his hopes up too high. Sierra wasn't a trained K9, and there were dozens of places this guy could have gone. As Sierra trotted past several on-street parking spaces, he wondered if the gunman had left a car nearby. It would explain how Kaleb had lost him so quickly.

That theory didn't pan out as Sierra turned another corner, then came to a stop in front of a small video game store. She sat staring up at him, so he dropped to his knees, wincing as the injured one protested, and praised her.

"Good girl, you're a good girl!"

Charlotte frowned at the store. "You really think he went inside here?"

"That's what Sierra is telling us." He rose to his feet. "But without a picture of this guy, we can't ask if any of the employees recognize him."

"We could ask if Thomas Acker works here." She shrugged. "I realize it's not likely, but it can't hurt."

He considered her suggestion. Tommy had enjoyed playing video games, so it was possible the kid's father, if that's who they were chasing down, may have been in here before to buy him things. "Let me try something else first." He turned toward Sierra. "Come."

The dog followed him as he went down the street until he found a side street that led down to a narrow alley. From there, he could see there were several back doorways along with a few dumpsters. Most places had a rear exit where employees came in and garbage was taken out, and he'd noticed the video game store was next to a small restaurant.

Charlotte followed, easily keeping up. He felt bad she often had to run to keep pace with them, but he didn't want to hold Sierra back when she was on the scent.

Staying on the side street, with the alley a few paces ahead, he offered Sierra the scent bag. "Seek!"

The canine lifted her nose to the air, then sniffed along the ground. She made another circle, and his hope deflated when she didn't immediately go to the alley. He kept his emotions in check, though. He'd read enough training manuals that dogs could pick up on their handler's emotions and could falsely alert just to please them.

And to get their own reward.

For a moment, he thought Sierra would head back toward the front of the video store, but she abruptly turned and trotted down toward the alley. She picked up speed when she took the alley toward the doorways. To his surprise, she stopped at one door, sniffed along the ground for a long moment, then sat and stared up at him.

"Good girl!" He pulled the tennis ball from his pocket and tossed it in the air. Sierra eagerly jumped up to grab it.

"I don't understand," Charlotte said. "Why would she alert here?"

"I think the guy in the knit cap went through the store, one which he probably knows well, escaping out the back. It was a good tactic as there are so many businesses along here, I had no way of knowing which one he'd chosen."

Sierra brought the ball back and dropped it at his feet. He picked it up and tossed it up for her again.

"Do you think she'll continue following the scent?" Charlotte asked.

"I hope so." He tossed the ball one more time, praising her again, before putting it away. "Seek Bad Man!"

Sierra didn't hesitate to go back to the door she'd just alerted on. Kaleb stared at her without offering a reward, so she went back to sniffing the ground, then headed the rest of the rest of the way down the alley. When they reached the busy street, he took Charlotte's hand.

"Stay close," he advised.

Sierra wound around several pedestrians but continued moving along the scent path. At least, he hoped that's what she was doing. When the dog came to another intersection, she turned to the right and stopped near a parking area. There was a car in the space, but she didn't care. She sniffed along the ground and then sat and stared up at him expectantly.

"Don't tell me he had a car," Charlotte said on a weary sigh.

"It seems so." He took out the tennis ball and drew Sierra away from the road before tossing it in the air. Then he swept his gaze over the location. "I'm sure there are cameras on those traffic lights over there. And probably on several of these businesses too."

Charlotte lifted a hand. "So what? We can't get access to the video without Grimes's help. And he's already gone out on a limb for us."

"I know, but we have to ask him to do more." He played with Sierra for a few minutes, ignoring the grumbles from a few pedestrians that gave them a wide berth. "Sierra followed this guy's scent. That should count for something."

"To us? Yes. To Detective Grimes? Doubtful."

Kaleb knew she might be right, especially because Sierra wasn't a police dog. But that didn't stop him from pulling out his cell phone. "Grimes? It's Tyson. Sierra followed the scent from the knit hat; we know the path the perp took yesterday. And there are plenty of cameras nearby that likely caught him on video."

"Tyson, you're a pain in my backside," Grimes said curtly. "I told you the hat can't be considered evidence as it could have been dropped by anyone. And your dog isn't a trained K9."

"What if she was?" Kaleb asked. "I mean, let's just say that you had a K9 cop on your team that followed the trail of this knit hat to a video store, then from the back door of a video store to a parking space across from a pizza joint. Are you saying that wouldn't be enough to search the video? For a man who shot at the same safe house on two separate occasions?"

Grimes didn't answer for a long moment. "Which pizza joint?"

Kaleb gave him the restaurant name and the address.

"I'll see what I can do but don't hold your breath," Grimes warned. "Most places around here don't cooperate with the police about viewing their security video without a search warrant."

"And you can't ask for a search warrant, why?"

"Because you're a civilian, and your dog could be following the scent of pizza for all I know," Grimes shot back. "Is that all? I have work to do."

"Yeah, that's all." Kaleb slipped his phone back into his pocket.

"He's not buying it?" Charlotte asked.

"I think he wants to but feels as if he doesn't have enough to follow police procedure." He stared at the camera above the traffic light. It made him long for the days he was overseas and didn't have to follow annoying rules like getting search warrants.

Then again, back in Afghanistan, they didn't have the luxury of cameras all over the city either.

"Now what?" Charlotte's expression was full of disappointment.

"We should head back to the new safe house location." He empathized with her dejection as he felt it too. "Unfortunately, there isn't anything more we can do here. I'll call for a rideshare." He pulled out his phone to find the app, but she put a restraining hand on his arm.

"Wait. What if you ask the restaurant workers to see their video? You're a handsome guy, I'm sure any woman would be more than willing to help you out."

She thought he was handsome? He tried hard not to grin. "I'll see what I can do, if you agree to do the same."

"Me?" She frowned.

"You're pretty and adorable, I'm sure any man would be willing to help you out," he said, tossing her words back at her. He took her hand. "Come on, we'll try the pizza joint first."

"You're crazy," she muttered, following him to the traffic light. Sierra stayed close too.

Through the window he could see the only employee was female. He handed Sierra's leash to her. "I guess I'm up."

The woman manning the cash register brightened when she saw him. "Hello. Can I help you?"

"Yes. I'm Navy SEAL Kaleb Tyson, and I'm following up on a shooting incident not far from here." He smiled. "I noticed you have a camera outside, pointed across the street. Would you mind if I reviewed it?"

"A Navy SEAL?" She looked impressed. "Thank you for your service."

He inclined his head. "It's an honor and a privilege."

Her smile faded as she tapped her finger on the computer. "I'm not supposed to share the store video," she said. "We have an arrangement with the restaurant across the street. We only share the video with each other, in case one of us is robbed. And the police if they provide a search warrant. This is private property, you know. We are under no obligation to release our video to anyone."

Interesting to learn about the second camera, but this one provided the best angle to view the driver's side door. "I understand, and I wouldn't ask if it wasn't for the fact that several women and children are in danger." He eased forward, holding her gaze. "Please? I would really appreciate it."

"Women and children?" She frowned, then shrugged.

"Okay." She capitulated quicker than he'd anticipated. "Hold on a minute." She hit a few keys on the computer, then turned the screen just enough for him to see it. "What time did you say?"

"Run the tape starting at one in the afternoon yesterday." He had no idea when the guy in the knit cap had parked the car, or how long he'd been hanging around outside the safe house. The bus had arrived at 3:00 p.m., so he hoped two hours beforehand was enough time. "I'm sorry, I didn't catch your name."

"Linda Kramer." She blushed and hit the play button. The video started, moving at normal time.

Since he didn't have two hours or more to watch it, he gestured to the screen. "Linda, do you mind if I fast-forward it?"

"Come over on this side," she invited.

He was hoping she'd say that. He hurried around the counter to join her at the computer. Taking over the keyboard, he increased the speed of the video.

When he saw the first car park in the spot, he realized the driver was a woman. Twenty minutes later, she left, and another vehicle slid into the spot. An older man with white hair got out from behind the wheel. He increased the speed again, going through several more vehicles until 2:35 when a black SUV pulled in and a man wearing a dark knit hat slid out from the driver's seat.

He froze the video, trying to capture the guy's face. But the street traffic made that difficult. He couldn't get a single decent view of the guy's face.

"Is that him?" Linda asked, leaning forward to see better.

"I believe so, yes." There was no sign of a weapon, but

that didn't mean much. The guy wore a black jacket and black jeans.

"Despicable," Linda said with a sniff.

"Yes, ma'am." When the guy was no longer in view, he sped up the video until the point the guy returned. As before, though, there wasn't a good view of his face. But he could see the guy's black hair. The guy had turned up the edges of his jacket to cover the sides of his face. Still, he froze the video. "Linda, would you mind if I print a copy of this?"

"Uh, sure. The printer is in the back room." She headed that way, returning a few minutes later. "It's not a great view of his face."

"I know. But it's better than nothing." He took the sheet of paper. "You've been very helpful, Linda. Thanks so much."

"Oh, well, anything to protect women and children."

When he returned outside, he handed the photograph to Charlotte. "The only thing this proves is that the guy who lost the knit cap resembles the dark-haired guy you and I saw the night before."

Charlotte looked at the image. "There's something familiar about him, like maybe I've seen him before I even realized he was following me. Yet I still can't say for sure this is Thomas Acker."

"I know. Not only is this street busy with traffic, but this guy was smart enough to keep his head down, using the edge of his jacket and the passing cars to hide his profile. There's another camera in the shop across the street, but I don't think that angle will help us. This was our best opportunity to get a clear look at his face."

"I was hoping for more," Charlotte admitted with a sigh. "Should we give this to Detective Grimes?"

"Yeah, I'll do that. Maybe it's enough of a likeness that he'll go after the other videos in the area. The traffic light video is high enough that it may show more, only because it's at a higher angle." He put his arm around her shoulders in a brief hug. "I know this doesn't seem like much, but it's a good lead."

"I know." She rested her head on his shoulder, leaning into his embrace. He swallowed hard, holding himself back from kissing her again.

"We—uh, should go." He found it difficult to think clearly when she was in his arms. But they'd been in the city long enough. They could go to more businesses to ask for video, but that would take time. Besides, he believed the traffic light video would be their best option for getting either a better view of the guy's face or the license plate number for his SUV.

His phone rang. Charlotte moved away so he could answer it. His pulse kicked up when he saw Grimes's name. "Tyson."

"We got a confirmation that the bullet pried out of the safe house was fired from a thirty-eight," Grimes said.

Kaleb tried not to show his frustration. "That's what we suspected."

"Yeah, well, I can't take assumptions to the judge for a warrant," Grimes answered testily. "Proof matters."

"I have something for you, a screenshot taken from the video at the pizza joint. I'll text you a copy, although there wasn't a clear view of his face, only confirmation that the guy who lost the knit hat has dark hair and somewhat resembles the mug shot you showed us."

"Why are you looking at video?" Grimes snapped. "I told you I'd work on it."

"I know, but we were able to sweet-talk our way in

without getting a warrant." He put the call on speaker so he could capture the image on his phone. He texted it to Grimes. "I was hoping this might be enough to get access to the traffic camera. As you can see, Sierra followed the suspect, just as I told you."

"Stay out of my case," Grimes grumbled. "I'll be in touch."

"Okay, but . . ." There was no use. He was talking to dead air. He put his phone away. It didn't matter that Grimes was upset with them as long as the detective continued to come up with leads.

He felt certain the photo he'd obtained would be the first step in getting the answers they desperately needed.

---

CHARLOTTE WAS IMPRESSED with the work Sierra and Kaleb had done. Tracking the guy's scent, getting a picture—granted, not a great one—of the gunman was amazing. As they took a rideshare back to the fancy house Kaleb had rented for them, she felt hopeful that the gunman would soon be found and tossed in jail.

"This must be costing you a fortune," she said after they emerged from the rideshare vehicle.

"Nah, all for a good cause." He shrugged off her concern. They headed up to the front door, and he quickly entered the key code. When they stepped inside, he turned to look at the alarm system, frowning when the red light wasn't on. "Why isn't the alarm activated?"

"I don't know." She glanced around, but Kaleb caught her hand, tugging her back.

"Stay behind me." Kaleb pulled his weapon and moved forward.

She stayed close as he moved farther into the house. The women and children inside were her responsibility, not Kaleb's. And how could the gunman have found them there? She felt certain one of the kids had gone outside and Milly had deactivated the alarm, forgetting to turn it back on.

"Kaleb? What's wrong?" Charlotte heard the panic in Milly's voice, no doubt upon seeing the gun in his hand.

"You didn't remember to set the alarm code," Kaleb said, his tone curt.

"I'm so sorry," Milly apologized. "Tommy went out, and I quickly got him back inside and meant to activate the alarm, but then Angela started crying, and I got distracted..." The older woman shot Kaleb an apologetic glance. "I'll do better next time."

"I know." He didn't scold her, but Charlotte could tell he'd expected more from Milly, and the other women as well.

"This place doesn't feel like a safe house to them," she said in a low voice. "Especially the kids. Remember, the windows were too high for them to see out at our previous safe house."

"It's fine. Just . . .worrisome," he admitted. "I'm glad they're safe. Stay here, I'm going to do another perimeter check with Sierra." He turned and headed to the door.

Charlotte turned toward Milly who looked crushed. "He's really mad at me."

"No, he's not." Charlotte patted Milly's arm. "He wants us to be safe."

"I'm not used to activating an alarm," Milly confessed. "I feel so safe here in this nice neighborhood without it."

"I know, it's so different, it feels like we're living on

another planet." Charlotte headed into the kitchen. "Do you need help with dinner?"

"No, I changed my mind about the pot roast and made lasagna instead." Her expression brightened. "Kaleb likes Italian food, maybe this will help smooth things over."

"I'm sure it will." Charlotte had to admit it was strange that she'd never seen Kaleb angry. Even in the early days of her relationship with Jerry, he'd lost his temper, hitting the table or the door frame. Looking back, she realized that should have been her first clue. Along with his annoyance over small ridiculous things, like her rain boots being left on the mat by the door or the dishes not getting done until the following day.

Yeah, she'd been blind and stupid all right. Despite those early clues, she'd never anticipated his fist pounding into her face, sending her flying onto her backside.

Followed by a kick to her ribs.

She shook off the painful and humiliating memories. Jerry was back in Minneapolis with his wife, Darla. Charlotte had sent an anonymous letter to the woman, warning her of Jerry's temper and his physical abuse. She only hoped Darla had figured it out before experiencing the abuse herself. There was a possibility, albeit a very slim one, that Jerry had learned his lesson and had found a way to control his temper.

"Charlotte?" Emma came into the room, wearing a midriff-baring, short-sleeved top and skintight leggings. She looked around anxiously. "Where's Kaleb? Did he stay in the city?"

"No, he's outside with Sierra." The sun was shining, but the air was still cool, and she could see the goosebumps along the woman's arms. "Get some clothes on, Emma. Kaleb is forty, that's old enough to be your father."

A flash of hurt flickered in the young woman's gaze. "He doesn't look forty. He's smokin' hot."

Charlotte privately agreed. Kaleb was by far the most handsome guy she'd ever kissed. She felt her cheeks flush and hoped Emma didn't notice. "He's here to protect us from harm, nothing more. As soon as the gunman is arrested, Kaleb will be on his way."

"Maybe he'll stay in the area," Emma protested. The young woman grimaced and reluctantly added, "He seems to like you."

"Don't be silly." Did he? He had kissed her, but that didn't mean much to some guys. Especially one as handsome as Kaleb. Better not to read too much into it. "Remember, Emma, Kaleb only came to the safe house in the first place to find Ava. She's been missing for several weeks now."

"I don't remember Ava."

"You came after she left." Charlotte could tell Emma was stalling, hoping Kaleb would return in time to see her. It was times like this that Charlotte felt every one of her thirty-seven years, and then some. "Go on, Emma. Dinner will be ready soon."

Emma slowly turned as the front door opened, revealing Kaleb and Sierra. He took a moment to activate the alarm, and when he turned back, there was no mistaking the pained expression in his eyes when he saw Emma.

"Kaleb, I was so worried about you." Emma sauntered closer. "I'm glad you made it home safe."

"Thanks, but this is a temporary safe house, not a home, something you and the others need to remember. And Charlotte and I were fine, we didn't run into any problems." He locked gazes with Charlotte, silently begging for help.

"Kaleb, do you have a minute? I need to talk to you

about Detective Grimes." It was the first thing that popped into her head.

"Of course. Please excuse us, Emma." He gave the young woman a wide berth and came over to take Charlotte's arm. Together, they walked through the living room and into the study located off on the opposite side of the house from the pool.

"Thanks for the rescue," Kaleb said in a low tone.

Charlotte winced when she heard Emma thudding up the stairs and slamming one of the bedroom doors behind her. "You're welcome, but you're kinda breaking her heart."

"What? No way! She's young enough to be my daughter!" Kaleb protested.

Charlotte smirked. "I told her that, but she doesn't care because you're '*smokin' hot*.'"

Kaleb rolled his eyes. "Whatever. She should know better than to flirt like that with someone she barely knows. Why is she so trusting of men anyway? I thought most of the residents here would rather avoid strangers like me."

"Emma was at first, but now I think she's in denial about what really happened. From the beginning she's chafed at the rules, claiming that Rodney was sorry for hurting her and that she probably overreacted by calling the police." She shrugged. "Maybe she wants to use you to make Rodney jealous. Or maybe she's over Rodney and looking for someone new. Either way, I have the impression she won't be staying with us for long."

"I get that vibe too," Kaleb admitted. "I'm sorry if she's upset."

"She's young, she'll get over it." At least, Charlotte hoped so. "Milly made lasagna for dinner, she's hoping that will help you forgive her."

"I'm not mad," he insisted. "But when I head into town tomorrow, you'll have to stay here to keep an eye on things."

"Tomorrow?" She frowned. "Why are you heading back?"

Before Kaleb could answer, the loud screech of the alarm system bounced off the walls.

"Get down," he shouted, pulling his gun and sprinting toward the front door. Charlotte didn't remain behind because she knew what had happened.

And she was right. The front door was open, and Emma was walking away, rolling her small bright pink suitcase behind her.

## CHAPTER EIGHT

———————————

"Should I haul her back here?" Kaleb glanced at Charlotte.

"No." Charlotte put a hand on his arm. "I've told you before, this isn't a jail. These women must choose to stay here. We don't force them to."

"Yeah, but . . ." He ground his teeth in frustration. "I'm the one who hurt her feelings. Maybe I can talk her into staying."

"You can try." Charlotte dropped her hand. "But don't give her false hope about having a future together. That would be worse for her in the long run."

"I won't." He rushed through the doorway, Sierra joining him. "Emma? Wait. Can we talk for a minute?"

Emma ignored him, holding her head high as she continued walking down the road. He wondered where she was planning to go. Did she have money? He could give her some additional cash if he couldn't convince her to return.

"Emma, please." Ignoring the pain in his right knee, he ran until he was close enough to grab her suitcase.

"Hey! Let go." She tried to tug it away from him.

He tightened his grip. "Look, I'm sorry if I hurt your

feelings. I care about you and the other women and kids. I want you all to be safe."

Emma avoided his gaze. "I'll be fine. Rod isn't a bad guy."

"Men who hit don't just stop, Emma. You've seen what those other women and their children have gone through. What makes you think Rod is different?"

"He loves me." Now her gaze was defiant.

"Then why did he hit you? Talk is cheap, Emma. It's easy to say he loves you, but his actions are what matter."

A flash of uncertainty darkened her gaze. "Whatever. I don't want to be stuck in a safe house. I want to live my life. Is that so difficult to understand?"

"No, of course not." Kaleb sensed he was losing her. "But isn't part of the process getting a safe place to live along with a new job? Why not give it some time?"

Emma propped one hand on her hip. "I can get my own job. And I have friends I can stay with. Charlotte said I could leave any time."

He reluctantly released his grip on her suitcase and dug in his pocket. He took out five twenty-dollar bills and held them out to her. "Okay, I know we can't force you to stay. Take care of yourself, Emma. I hope you don't get hurt again."

"I won't." She hesitated, staring at the money, then took the twenties, stuffing them into the pocket of her skintight jeans. "Thanks."

He turned away, hoping she'd follow, but she didn't. By the time he reached the front door and looked back over his shoulder, Emma was out of sight. With a sigh, he punched in the key code, then went inside. After reactivating the alarm, he went to find Charlotte, following the enticing scent of lasagna into the kitchen.

"I couldn't get Emma to change her mind," he said.

"You tried, that's what counts." Charlotte sighed. "I'm a little surprised she lasted this long."

"That's only because she was hoping Kaleb would make a move," Milly said. "The girl is too bold for her own good."

Kaleb privately agreed. "Something smells incredible, Milly."

"Lasagna and garlic bread." Milly wrapped long loaves of bread in foil, then slid the tray into the oven. "It will be ready in ten minutes."

"I'll get the residents," Charlotte said.

He washed his hands in the sink, then took a moment to feed Sierra. As she ate, he turned toward Milly. "Anything I can do to help?"

"No thank you." Milly gave him a hesitant smile. "I'm really sorry about forgetting to set the alarm."

"Hey, it's fine. Everyone is safe, right?" Well, except maybe for Emma, but that was her choice, one she was responsible for.

All he could do was pray for her safety.

"Yes." Milly frowned. "But if something bad had happened, I'd never forgive myself."

"We're all human, Milly. We make mistakes. We have to forgive others and ourselves, the way Jesus taught us to."

The older woman regarded him thoughtfully. "Thank you, Kaleb. That's a nice way to think about forgiveness."

Before he could respond further, Charlotte returned with several of the women. He noticed she was staying close to Willow and Tommy, maybe because it was highly likely that Thomas Acker was the man who'd fired at the safe house.

After they all settled into the dining room, he bowed his

head to silently say grace. When he lifted his head, he caught them all staring at him.

"Maybe you should pray out loud," Milly suggested.

"Of course." He smiled. "Lord, we ask You to bless this food, bless these people seeking refuge, and please continue to keep them all safe in Your loving care. Amen."

"Amen," Milly said.

"Amen," Charlotte added.

There was a brief silence while the rest of the women and children glanced at each other as if unsure what to do. "Dig in," he said, lightening the somber tone. "We never let good food go to waste, right?"

"Right," Tommy agreed, reaching for the garlic bread.

"I can't believe Emma left," one of the women said.

"Everyone has to make their own choices," Charlotte reminded gently. "We can't make them for her."

"I know, but why leave when we're here in the best place ever?" another woman asked. "I mean, even if I did want to leave, I wouldn't go now. This place is the bomb!"

Kaleb held back from giving his own opinion. This wasn't his area of expertise, and it seemed as if Charlotte and Milly had dealt with this before.

Like when Ava had left. He frowned, realizing he hadn't given much thought to Ava or Nico or any of the other members of the team. He waited until they were finished eating before taking his phone into the other room to call Nico.

"Find anything?" Nico asked.

"No, but I hope you got my message about Simon having a different last name."

"I did, yeah. It's not very helpful, though. I'm not finding much intel under either name, Simon Marks or

Simon Normandy." Nico sounded frustrated. "For all we know, they're both fake. Where are you?"

"Still in LA. There's a security situation I need to deal with."

"Okay, there isn't much else I can do now anyway. I followed up with the last known address of Simon Normandy, but it's an empty apartment. No forwarding address."

That wasn't good news. "I'm sorry, Nico."

"Me too. But hey, the only easy day was yesterday, right? Something will turn up, you'll see."

Kaleb admired his buddy's positive attitude. "Let me know if you need something more. I'm hoping to finish up this job by the end of the week."

"Job? As in a paid assignment?" Nico asked.

"Not exactly." Kaleb had to grin since this situation was quite the opposite. He'd paid for this safe house, and the charter bus, and the rideshares back and forth. "I'm keeping some women and kids safe, Nico. I know Jay would want us to find Ava, but he wouldn't want these women in danger either."

"No, he wouldn't," Nico agreed. "Hey, have you heard from Hudd? He's been off-grid for the past eight weeks, and Senior Chief and the others are getting worried."

"Not yet."

"You're his swim buddy, Kaleb. I thought for sure he'd reach out to you over the others."

"I know." Mason's original swim buddy had rung the bell, dropping out of BUD/S training. Mason had been assigned a new swim buddy, but they'd ended up going on different teams after Mason had been promoted to Senior Chief. Dallas and Dawson had been buddied up together, and Nico and Jaydon had also been swim buddies. He and

Hudson had been inseparable back then. "I don't understand why Hudd feels the need to go it alone."

"Me either," Nico agreed.

Not good. "I'll try him again, maybe he'll eventually reach out."

"Okay, keep in touch, bro." Nico disconnected from the call.

He left a message, claiming he needed backup. Hudson's silence was troubling. As a team, they'd each covered each other's backs almost every day. Kaleb wanted to be there for Hudd too. But he couldn't leave LA. Not until he knew the dark-haired guy was behind bars.

The rest of the evening passed without incident. The way Charlotte kept herself busy gave him the impression she was avoiding him.

He told himself to get over it.

Finally, the women and children disappeared upstairs. He wondered if their sleeping arrangements would change now that Emma was gone, but he didn't ask. His job was to make sure no one got into the house, much less all the way upstairs to their bedrooms.

"Ready to go outside, girl?" Kaleb went to the door, keyed in the code, and opened the door. He quickly reactivated the alarm, then began his routine of checking the perimeter. Only he went counterclockwise this time, varying his routine as he'd been taught during SEAL training.

As he went around the back, he heard voices coming from the road. Two women arguing over plans for the weekend. He crept forward, glad to see them get into their car and drive away. Nodding in satisfaction, he returned to his job of securing the property.

Once Sierra took care of business, he continued moving

through the backyard. The surface of the pool glimmered under the city lights, reminding him of how the kids had splashed and played earlier that afternoon.

Enjoying themselves, the way kids ought to.

After reassuring himself the area was safe, he led Sierra inside. The main level was mostly dark, except for one light in the kitchen. He headed to the too-short sofa and stretched out, patting the floor beside him.

This time, when he finally fell asleep, he didn't have the reoccurring nightmare. A thudding sound abruptly woke him. He sat upright, blinking in the darkness while straining to listen.

One of the women upstairs? Or someone outside?

Sierra was sitting and staring at the front door, so he stuffed his feet into his shoes and pulled his Sig Sauer from beneath the pillow. Being a SEAL had taught him nothing good happened at three in the morning, and it was about that time now. He went to the windows overlooking the pool, scanning the yard for signs of an intruder.

"Kaleb?" Charlotte's whisper broke the silence. "What was that?"

"Not sure." He glanced over at her, not surprised she was standing in the middle of the stairway, holding her gun in both hands. "Stay here, I'll go outside to check it out."

"Why not wait to see if the alarm is breeched?" She didn't stay where she was, she came the rest of the way down the stairs and crossed over to him. "I'd rather you stay in here with us."

"Hey, you're a force to be reckoned with," he reminded her. "I'll leave Sierra with you, if that makes you feel better."

She nibbled on her lower lip, then shook her head. "No, take her with you. You need backup."

"I'm sure it's nothing." He turned to Sierra. "Come."

Sierra eagerly came to stand next to him as if anxious to get outside. He deactivated the alarm, slipped outside, then punched in the code. He silently moved around to the side of the building opposite from the swimming pool. Sierra blended into the shadows beside him.

Another thudding sound, then the rustling of leaves. Was the intruder leaving? Kaleb frowned and silently moved closer, his gaze trying to pick up the movement.

There!

A tall, dark shadow ran from beneath a trio of palm trees, darting through the backyard of the house next door. Kaleb picked up his pace rather than giving Sierra the attack command. What if this was just a neighborhood kid messing around? He didn't want to be responsible for injuring an innocent person. Especially since he didn't see how their safe house location could have been found by the dark-haired guy.

"Stop! You're trespassing on private property!"

The shadow didn't stop; instead, it put on a burst of speed. Kaleb jumped over a scrubby bush, wincing when his knee twinged at the impact.

By the time he reached the property line, the shadow was gone.

---

CHARLOTTE FOUND herself holding her breath as she waited for Kaleb and Sierra to investigate the source of the thudding sound. When her chest grew unbearably tight, she forced herself to exhale and breathe normally.

Kaleb was a highly trained, incredibly smart Navy

SEAL. She couldn't ask for a better protector. Sierra, too, would keep him safe.

The seconds ticked by with agonizing slowness. She moved from one window to the next, but she didn't see Kaleb or Sierra. She told herself Kaleb was used to hiding from the enemy, but she couldn't relax.

Although she could pray. Something she hadn't done until Kaleb had come into her life. She cleared her throat and whispered, "Lord, Kaleb is one of Your children. Please keep him safe in Your care!"

In the back of her mind, she heard, *You are one of My children too.* The thought had her going still.

Was it true? That even though she hadn't prayed before, was she still one of God's children?

Were all the women and children she'd housed over the years His children too?

A noise at the front door distracted her from the revelation. She hurried over in time to see Kaleb come through the door.

"Did you find anything?" She watched as he came inside and reactivated the alarm.

"There was someone out there, but he took off." Kaleb's expression was grim. "I didn't send Sierra after him because I was afraid the intruder might just be one of the neighborhood kids goofing around."

"I understand." She blew out a sigh. "The good news is that you scared him off. If it was just a kid, he won't make the mistake of coming back here again."

"I hope not." Kaleb walked into the living room and slid his weapon beneath his pillow. Then he looked back at her. "How did you hear the noise anyway?"

She flushed. "For some reason, I'm not sleeping well. I

was debating coming down to make tea, but I didn't want to wake you up again. Then I heard the noise."

"I'm surprised you came down with your gun," he said with a frown. "You know I would give my life to protect you and the others."

She nodded. His statement was made so easily, but she knew he meant it. Other men might say something similar, but then they didn't stick around when things spiraled out of control.

Or they saved themselves rather than protecting others.

"You need some Sleepytime tea." Kaleb moved toward the kitchen.

Charlotte followed more slowly, acutely aware of the last time she and Kaleb had been alone in the kitchen at night. Just thinking about Sleepytime tea brought back memories of his incredible kiss.

Yet heading back upstairs to the bedroom she shared with Milly wasn't something she was ready to do either. Why was she having so much trouble sleeping? This location was probably the safest one they'd been in recently.

No reason to overreact to every unusual sound.

"Here you go." Kaleb handed her the box of tea.

"Thanks." She skirted around him to fill a mug with water. "I guess you're right about the noise coming from a neighborhood kid. I'm sure Sierra would have given you some indication if she'd picked up the scent of the dark-haired man."

"Maybe, but you've given me an idea." He returned to the sofa, coming up with the bag containing the knit cap. "Enjoy your tea, we'll be back soon."

She frowned as Kaleb once again went outside with Sierra. Interesting that he was always careful to turn the alarm system on and off, as if he'd lived with one before.

Something to think about if they were able to return to their old safe house. Or for their new one, if they were forced to relocate. Which reminded her that she hadn't contacted Abby recently to give her an update. Charlotte made a mental note to update her wealthy donor later that morning.

When the microwave dinged, she removed her tea and sat at the counter. There was no reason to be nervous, she knew Kaleb was double-checking to make sure the guy he'd chased off wasn't the gunman who'd come after their previous safe house. And really, how could it be? There's no possible way their location could have been leaked.

Kaleb returned in less than ten minutes. "We need to call Detective Grimes."

"What? Why?" She searched his gaze. "Did Sierra alert outside?"

"Yes." Kaleb's expression was grim. "I'm such an idiot. I should have sent Sierra to take him down. She'd have caught easily caught him."

With trembling fingers, Charlotte set her tea aside. "I don't understand, Kaleb. How is it possible he found us here?"

"I don't know." Kaleb already had his phone out, scrolling through his contacts. "But I want Grimes to find out exactly where Thomas Acker is. Tommy's father must be the guy coming after you."

"But how?" She tried to think back to how they'd taken a rideshare to come here. Maybe the dark-haired man had noticed them outside the pizza place. She and Kaleb had walked another two blocks before getting a rideshare, but it was possible that he'd watched them get into the vehicle. But then, what? He'd run to his car stashed somewhere nearby, managing to find them and follow them here?

It just didn't seem likely.

"Detective, this is Kaleb Tyson. The dark-haired intruder has found our new safe house. Sierra picked up his scent in several spots outside, especially near some palm trees where I saw him too. I need you to call me back right away!" He stabbed the end call button and tossed the phone onto the counter, revealing his frustration.

"You're sure about Sierra picking up his scent?"

A flash of hurt crossed his eyes. "You saw her in action today, remember? She did the same thing tonight."

"I believe you," she hastened to reassure him. "But if that's the case, we can't stay here, Kaleb. Not if he knows our location."

"I thought of that," Kaleb admitted. "But we do have the alarm system. Maybe that's what stopped him from trying to get inside."

"He didn't hesitate to use a gun a few days ago," she pointed out. "Why stop now?"

Kaleb shook his head. "I don't know. I agree it doesn't seem logical. Unless his only goal was to check the place out, look for ways to get inside without being seen. Seeing the alarm system in place may have scared him off."

"I guess that makes sense." She couldn't suppress a shiver. She cradled her tea mug in her hands, drawing warmth from the mug.

An uneasy silence fell between them. The idea of packing everyone up again and moving to a new location in a matter of days was daunting. A tiny voice in the back of her mind screamed that it was unfair, but she knew that didn't matter. No one ever promised life would be fair.

She knew that better than most.

"Hey, it will be okay," Kaleb said gently.

"I know." She forced a smile, telling herself to buck up.

Feeling sorry for herself and for the women and children in her care was a waste of time and energy. "It's just frustrating the police can't catch this guy."

"I'm hoping this new incident will convince Grimes to push harder to find and question Thomas Acker," Kaleb said. "He's the most logical suspect."

She wanted to agree but couldn't shake the fact that the guy in the photo array wasn't the same one she'd glimpsed following her. The differences were so subtle she couldn't articulate them well enough to convince the detective.

When Kaleb's phone rang, they both jumped. Tea sloshed over the rim of her cup, making a mess.

"Hey, Grimes, thanks for calling me back. I'm putting this on speaker because Charlotte is with me." He placed the phone between them. "Please tell me you have something on Acker."

"Do you realize it's almost four in the morning?" Grimes sounded cranky. "We haven't found Acker yet, but I've issued a BOLO for him as a person of interest."

"Be on the lookout for," Kaleb explained as Charlotte gave a questioning look. "So you have no idea if he has an alibi for the time frame of either shooting or tonight?"

"Not yet, no. But how could he have found you, Tyson? I don't even know where you're staying."

"I think it's possible he saw us at the pizza place," Charlotte said. "Maybe because he'd returned to find his hat. If so, he could have easily watched us get into the rideshare vehicle and then jump into his own car to follow us here."

Kaleb grimaced. "I was careful to search for signs of a tail. I hate to think he's that good that I missed him."

"Yeah, well, what do you want me to do at this hour?" Grimes asked wearily. "I can put in a report of a prowler, but you'll have to give me your address. And as the place isn't in my jurisdiction, I'll need to alert those officers too."

She locked gazes with Kaleb. Was it worth giving their location away? She was surprised at the resounding no that echoed in the back of her mind.

"You should know that Sierra alerted on his scent, the same guy who lost his knit hat was outside this house. The sooner you find this guy, the better."

"The dog again, huh?"

"Yes. I'm sorry I woke you, Detective," Kaleb said. "I just wanted you to know that this guy is still out there, trying to get close to the women and children."

"Yeah, fine. I'll reinforce with the sergeant that Thomas Acker is a top priority. Good night." Grimes disconnected from the call.

"Thank you for not giving our address out," she said in a low voice. "I can't explain why, but I don't want it listed in a police report." She hesitated, then added, "It's a catch-22 situation. As an abuse victim, they won't arrest the abuser unless you agree to press charges. And doing that means you have to put all the details out there, which end up in a police report. Which the abuser then gets to see so that he can formulate an argument, denying the charges." She shook her head. "It's no wonder so many of these women don't bother."

Kaleb reached out to take her hand. "I'm sorry, that must have been horrible for you."

She nodded, clutching his hand tightly. "Jerry seemed so nice in the beginning. I never expected him to turn into a monster."

"Jerry sounds like a jerk, and I hope the cops tossed him in jail."

"Not for long." She avoided his gaze, staring at their

clasped hands instead. "That's the other way the system is wrong. These guys get out on a ridiculously low bond, then they can seek revenge against the women who pressed charges in the first place."

"Jerry did that?"

She nodded. "He shoved his way into my apartment, grabbed my hair, and hit my head on the counter." She finally dragged her gaze to his. "I was knocked out, but thankfully, the neighbor across the hall called the police. The sirens must have scared him off. After I woke up and was discharged from the hospital, I went to a safe house like this. From there, I moved across the country so that he could never find me."

Kaleb's gaze hardened. "He never did any jail time for hurting you?"

"No. Because being safe was more important." She abruptly pulled her hand from his and stood. "I have to go. Good night." She couldn't bear his intense gaze, so she turned and ran upstairs.

Like the coward Kaleb now knew she was.

# CHAPTER NINE

Staring at his clenched fists, Kaleb forced himself to remain calm. Charlotte's story was far worse than he'd imagined. He wasn't a violent man by nature, but if Jerry walked in now, he would be tempted to slug him, hard, just so that the lowlife jerk would understand exactly how it felt.

Violence wasn't the answer. Jesus would not condone that behavior. Yet the images of what Charlotte described flashed over and over in his head, filling him with a helpless fury.

He couldn't help but wonder if the reason she'd cut her hair was because of what that jerk did to her. Sierra bumped her head against his side, looking up at him. She could sense his tumultuous emotions, so he leaned over to reassure her.

"I'm fine." He wasn't, but he did his best to let go of the anger. There wasn't anything he or Charlotte could do to change the past. Admirable that she'd turned around to dedicate her life to helping other women.

Women and children who'd suffered what she had.

Kaleb rose and headed into the living room. If he kept

thinking about Charlotte lying unconscious on the floor, he'd never be able to sleep. Or to focus on the dark-haired guy who had been outside.

When Sierra had alerted near the palm trees, he'd wondered if it was a false positive. He knew Sierra wanted to please him, and the possibility of the gunman finding them all the way out here seemed impossible.

He hadn't rewarded her but took her around the other side of the house, where the pool and patio were located. He gave her the scent bag again, telling her to seek the bad man, and she eagerly went to work. But she did not alert in that area.

Working their way around the house, Sierra had alerted near a window looking into the office and then again near the palm trees. He'd rewarded her with the tennis ball, his mind whirling.

He hated thinking he may have inadvertently led this guy here. Although he really didn't see how. Charlotte had a point about them being seen at the pizza joint, but following their rideshare seemed a stretch.

Nothing was impossible, though. His SEAL training had taught him that. The things they'd endured had pushed them to their limits, yet they'd not only survived, they'd thrived.

*Never underestimate the enemy.*

Okay, then. He'd assume the worst, that the dark-haired gunman had been outside the house. Kaleb and Sierra had chased him off, but he might return. Getting shut-eye was out of the question. He stood and moved from one window to the other, trying to come up with a way to trap this guy.

A house this large made that difficult. There were so many windows he could shoot at. So many places he could attempt to breach. The alarm would put Kaleb and the women on notice, but it wouldn't provide the specific location since the alarm system wasn't updated to modern technology standards.

Allowing this guy to breach the house wasn't an option.

Kaleb rummaged through the kitchen drawers, looking for anything useful. There was duct tape but nothing else. The house had a finished basement, a large recreational room with a large-screen TV to watch movies. He rushed through there to the back utility area and hit pay dirt. There were some tools, but even better, some fishing gear. A tackle box containing several yards of fishing line, fishing hooks, and a large net.

Perfect.

He hauled everything upstairs and quickly cut the net away from the pole. Then he cut several lengths of fishing line, tucked the hooks into his pocket, and grabbed the duct tape.

"Sierra, stay. Guard." He couldn't take her outside with him for this job, she'd only get in the way, and he didn't want to risk her being injured. Kaleb disabled the code, stepped outside, and then keyed the alarm back on.

He worked as quickly as possible. Daylight was only a couple of hours away. Still, he wasn't going to assume this guy wouldn't try again. Daytime hadn't stopped him before, no reason to think it would again. Kaleb set up several low trip wires with the fishing line, then used the duct tape to make a sling, and used two hooks to help suspend the net beneath the broad palm leaves. If the guy looked up, he'd see the net hanging there, but most people didn't do that. Especially if they were intent on creeping silently toward a house to wreak havoc. The sling would tug the wire that would release the net. Crude, but better than nothing.

The trip wires would be his best bet, so he strung a few

more along the back and near the front of the house too. Then he went to the darkest corner of the property, pressing himself against the side of the building, and sat down to wait.

It was chilly without having Sierra with him, sharing her body heat, but he ignored the discomfort. The neighborhood was surprisingly quiet, or maybe it was just that the properties were spaced far enough apart to make it difficult to overhear any conversations.

He personally preferred to have distance from others. He'd spent over twenty years bunking with teammates and living in what they often called the Sandbox, which was the desert in Afghanistan. He appreciated being back on US soil, but he didn't particularly want to mingle with a bunch of people.

Ironic, really, that he was here keeping a whole group of women and kids safe.

That thought led him back to Charlotte. His heart ached for her. Easy to understand now how she'd turned from God. It had been a difficult path for him, too, after their last op had gone sideways, killing Jaydon. But Kaleb also knew he wouldn't be here right now without God's love and grace.

The hours slipped by one by one. Dawn broke slowly over the horizon, a faint light at first, slowly growing brighter. Still, he stayed where he was, silently willing this guy to return so that he could grab him.

A noise to his right made him stiffen. He slowly rose, his right knee screaming in pain after being in one position for so long. Keeping his back pressed against the wall, he continued to listen.

"Kaleb? Are you okay?" Charlotte's hushed whisper made him grimace.

"Fine, stay back. I don't want you to get hurt." He took a moment to sweep his gaze over the area before carefully making his way to the front door.

"Did you stay out there all night?" Charlotte's face was pale, dark circles marring her eyes.

"Just since you went to bed." He urged her inside, then activated the alarm. He bent to pet Sierra, who acted as if he'd been gone for a week rather than three and a half hours. "You and the others can't walk around outside, Charlotte. I've set up some traps in case this guy returns."

"Traps?" she echoed, her aquamarine eyes widening in shock. "What do you mean?"

"Trip wires, mostly. Nothing that's going to hurt him." Not that he was overly concerned about the dark-haired guy possibly being injured. "It's a way to make sure we can hear him coming before he has time to do something dangerous."

"Like shoot at us," Charlotte said grimly. "Smart of you to think of that."

"I need you to make sure none of the others go wandering around the property." He hesitated, then added, "I'm sorry, but we can't allow the kids to swim today either. That's a risk I'm not willing to take."

"I understand." She shook her head. "They'll be disappointed, of course, but keeping them safe is more important."

"It is, yes. I just feel bad that they have to suffer because of this guy." And he was once again mad at himself for letting him get away. "Excuse me while I take Sierra out."

Charlotte smiled at the dog. "She stood at the front door like a furry sentinel. I was worried she wouldn't let me go outside to find you."

"Yeah, we're a great team, but I left her inside so she wouldn't get caught in the trip wires." He went through the alarm routine to take her out for a bathroom break, then brought her inside.

Milly was up, based on the sounds coming from the kitchen. He took the opportunity to shower before returning to grab some badly needed coffee.

"We're having pancakes today," Milly announced. "As requested by the kids."

"No complaints from me." Kaleb sipped his coffee. "Did Charlotte let you know about the need to stay inside?"

"Yes." Milly's expression darkened. "It's a shame the police haven't arrested that man yet."

"We'll get him." He injected confidence into his tone. "Soon."

"Do you think we should continue staying here?" Charlotte asked. "I need to call my donor to make arrangements if we need to relocate."

He turned to glance at her. She'd showered, too, her short dark hair damp, curling slightly around her face. She was so adorable it took all his willpower not to sweep her into his arms. "I think we stay today. We need to give Detective Grimes the chance to get his hands on Thomas Acker."

"What about Tom?" Willow asked, coming into the room. Her fearful gaze bounced from him to Charlotte and back again. "You think he's the one doing this?"

"We don't know he's responsible," Charlotte said firmly. "Trust me, Willow, he's one of many suspects." She lifted a slip of paper. "I made a list of more names of abuse victims for the detective to follow up on. Please don't assume the worst, okay?"

"Okay." Willow's gaze remained skeptical, and Kaleb couldn't blame her.

"Don't say anything to Tommy," Kaleb added. "He

doesn't need to worry. I'm here, and I promise I won't let anything happen to either of you."

Willow nodded again, then turned away, no doubt to find her son. Kaleb could tell she was shaken by the news of her ex-husband being a likely suspect. The only positive side of the situation was that if Acker was responsible, he wouldn't get off with a slap on the wrist.

Kaleb would push hard to make sure he was charged for attempted murder.

"I wish I could believe Acker was the one responsible," Charlotte said in a low voice. "I know I only caught a brief glimpse of his face, but he didn't match up to the mug shot Detective Grimes showed us."

"I know." He was bothered by that too. "Maybe Acker did something to subtly alter his looks."

"Maybe." He could tell she didn't believe him. Kaleb wasn't entirely sure he believed it either.

He wanted, needed to get this guy.

"Breakfast will be ready in five minutes," Milly announced.

"Thanks, Milly." Charlotte stared at him for a long moment before joining her in the kitchen.

Kaleb walked from window to window, searching for signs of the intruder. But the area around the safe house remained undisturbed.

As he made his way back to join the group, he silently prayed for strength and patience, sensing he would need large doses of both to get through the rest of the day.

---

PHYSICALLY AND EMOTIONALLY EXHAUSTED, Charlotte did her best to put on a brave face for the women and children who were counting on her and Kaleb to keep them safe.

But it wasn't easy. Those moments she'd thought Kaleb had been hurt, or worse, had ravaged what little composure she'd had.

Logically, she should have expected him to be waiting outside for the dark-haired man to return. But the thought of losing him had struck hard.

Forcing her to realize how much she cared about him. Not just as someone who was kind enough to offer his protection but on a personal level.

Shaking her head at her own foolishness, she tried to focus on their next steps. Obviously, Kaleb wouldn't be heading back to their old safe house with Sierra to find more video of the gunman.

Yet depending solely on Detective Grimes didn't sit well either. He was doing his best, but he didn't have much to show for his efforts.

Charlotte barely remembered Kaleb saying grace or eating Milly's pancakes. There had been a series of protests after she'd informed the group there would be no swimming, but the kids had quickly agreed to Willow's idea of a movie session instead. It was a good plan to have the kids and the women stay down in the large rec room, away from the main level.

After breakfast was over, Milly nudged her out of the kitchen. "It's Tina's turn to wash dishes," Milly said firmly. "No offense, but you look awful. I know you didn't sleep much last night. You should take a nap, get some rest."

"Yeah, okay," she answered absently. But rather than heading back upstairs, she went in search for Kaleb instead.

"Something wrong?" He seemed concerned.

"Will you call Grimes? I'd like an update, and I have those additional names he'd asked for."

"Sure." He drew her into the study. "Although I don't know that he'll have much to tell us."

"I know." She rubbed her bloodshot eyes. "I need him to get to the bottom of this mess. The pressure is wearing me down."

"Hey, I'm here for you." Kaleb's dark gaze held sympathy. "I know how difficult it is for you to trust me, but I would die before I let anything happen to you or the others."

"I trust you, Kaleb. But I'm sure you can't just hang around here indefinitely."

"Yeah, I can." He drew her to the small sofa. "I'm here for as long as it takes."

*Until the next guy comes after us*, she thought on a sigh. Then she realized she was behaving badly. It wasn't like her to wallow in a puddle of self-pity. She lifted her chin and drew in a deep breath. "I need to give him the names I came up with."

Kaleb drew the phone from his pocket, found Grimes's number, put the call on speaker, and balanced the device on his thigh.

"Tyson, are you calling with new information?" Grimes asked.

"Detective, it's Charlotte. I would like to send you the names of the residents who stayed here over the last six months."

"That's fine. Can you take a picture and text it to me?"

"Of course." She looked at Kaleb who nodded encouragingly. "Do you have any news on Thomas Acker?"

"No." The blunt response made her cranky. "I told you

I'd let you know when I did. Calling me every few hours isn't going to make things happen any faster."

"The guy was here last night," Kaleb said. "I think it's reasonable to understand these women and children are afraid of what he'll try next."

She heard Grimes sigh. "I get that, but I'm doing my best. The BOLO has gone out, and the cops are actively looking for him."

"We know you are," Kaleb assured him.

"If you want to give me your address, I can let the locals know to keep an eye on your place," Grimes offered.

Charlotte locked her eyes on Kaleb and shook her head vehemently. He nodded in agreement.

"That's okay, I've got things covered here," Kaleb said. "Besides, technically, the only law he broke is trespassing on private property. I don't think that will be enough to convince the local police to do frequent patrols past the house."

"Up to you. Let me know if you change your mind," Grimes said. "Anything else?"

"Nothing from me," Charlotte admitted. "Thanks for your help, Detective."

"You're welcome." Grimes abruptly disconnected from the call.

She rubbed her aching temples. "I knew he wouldn't have any new information to share."

"Let's see that list of names." Kaleb held up his phone. "I'll text him the info."

After handing it over, she rose and crossed to the window. "I'm starting to wonder if we'll ever be safe again."

"You will be." Kaleb took the photo, sent the text, then came to stand beside her. "Whoever that guy is, he'll try again. And this time, I'll be ready for him."

"Okay." She told herself to get a grip. "Thanks, Kaleb."

"Anytime." There was a moment's pause before he asked, "Charlotte, I don't want to pry, but can I ask you something?"

Her stomach knotted as she lifted her gaze to his. She'd been wondering when he was going to ask again about why she didn't press charges against Jerry. She steeled herself to face his disappointment. "Of course."

"Does Jerry have dark hair?"

"Dark hair?" She frowned. "What? Oh, no." She flushed, belatedly realizing what Kaleb was getting at. "He has bright red hair, and I'm sure he's still in Minneapolis. The last time I looked him up, I discovered he'd gotten married." She couldn't help but grimace as the old familiar guilt kicked in. If she'd have stayed to press charges, Jerry may not have married Darla.

But, at the time, it had seemed like disappearing from the area, leaving the apartment where she'd lived for three years, was the only way to survive.

"He could have dyed it dark," Kaleb said.

A cold chill snaked down her spine. But then she shook her head. "He could, sure, but how would he have found me here in Los Angeles? It's not like I left a forwarding address. Minneapolis is thousands of miles away from here. And living at a safe house provides me additional cover."

Kaleb frowned. "Maybe."

"Really, it's not him. Why would Jerry bother to come after me? He's got a woman in his life to control, to abuse. There's certainly no need for him to track me down after all this time."

"How much time?" Kaleb pressed.

"Five years." In truth, it seemed like much longer. As if her life before California was nothing more than a foggy dream. And maybe it was. Charlotte knew she wasn't the same woman she was back then.

Thanks to Jerry, she'd morphed into someone else. Someone who knew the ugly side of life, faced it every day, and worked hard to protect others the way Sally and the women at the safe house she stayed at had protected her.

"What's Jerry's last name?"

"Schubert. But I truly don't think he's our guy. I'm sure I would have recognized him, even if he had dyed his hair."

"You're probably right, but I appreciate you giving me the information anyway." Kaleb's smile didn't quite reach his eyes. "In case I happen to end up in Minneapolis at some point."

"Don't, Kaleb." She frowned, lightly touching his arm. "You're a good man. Don't stoop to his level. He's not worth it."

Now his smile gentled, and he lightly brushed his finger down her cheek. "Okay, you're probably right. As much as I want to pummel him, I'll stay away. For you, Charlotte."

Her lips curved in a reluctant smile. "I used to imagine taking kickboxing classes just so I could punch him back, then I realized that was the wrong approach. Now I just hope that he'll do something that will land him in jail."

"Maybe he already has. We should pray for his wife," Kaleb said softly.

She was nodded, about to explain about the anonymous notes she'd sent, then she saw something move out the window. She grabbed his arm. "I think someone's out there."

"Stay here and keep everyone away from the windows. Sierra, guard!" Instantly, Kaleb had his weapon in hand and was heading for the front door.

Charlotte followed him out of the study. Sierra stayed

close to her side as she made a quick detour to the kitchen to find Milly. "We need to get into the basement rec room with the others."

"Okay." Milly didn't argue but thrust the ground meat she was thawing for lunch into the fridge and followed her down the stairs.

"What's going on?" Willow asked, looking at her sharply.

"Nothing, we're fine." Charlotte did her best to reassure them. "Just taking extra precautions. Milly, I need you and Willow to keep everyone down here. I'll be back soon."

"Where are you going?" Milly demanded.

She didn't want to tell them she was going to get her gun. "I need to check the alarm system. Don't worry, I won't be long. Stay here, no one goes upstairs, understand?"

Willow nodded, her eyes dark with fear. She tugged her son Tommy close to her side.

Milly eyed her suspiciously, likely knowing full well Kaleb would never forget to activate it, but she held her tongue. Milly was smart enough to figure out what Charlotte intended to do.

Better for Charlotte to be armed than Milly. Not only was the older woman not a very good shot, but she made it clear she didn't like using a gun.

Charlotte raced up the stairs to the main level, with Sierra accompanying her. Kaleb's dog stayed close to her side, which was reassuring. She felt certain the dog would attack anyone who threatened her. Maybe she should get a dog like Sierra after Kaleb left. It would be nice to have additional backup. She was sure Kaleb would tell her where he adopted Sierra and even give her tips on training the dog.

Time to consider that idea later. She entered the master

suite. Sierra seemed confused; she kept sitting in front of Charlotte as if to force her to stay put.

"This won't take long," she said to the dog, hoping the animal would calm down a bit. Apparently, the K9 took her command of guarding her seriously. No matter what Charlotte did, the dog attempted to sit right in front of her. A phenomenon that would have made her smile if the situation wasn't so grim.

Rummaging in the nightstand, she removed her .38. She always made sure to keep her gun away from the kids, trigger lock securely in place. Deep down, she didn't like guns either. She and Milly were similar in that way. But the difference was that Charlotte knew having a weapon was necessary. Hadn't that been proven by this dark-haired guy's actions? She couldn't afford to hesitate in doing what needed to be done.

With trembling fingers, she quickly removed the trigger lock and double-checked to make sure the weapon was loaded.

There wasn't a doubt in her mind that Kaleb would sacrifice his life if needed. After all, she planned to do the same thing. If Kaleb was the first line of defense, she would be the second.

She pulled a sweatshirt out of the closet and tucked the gun inside the pocket. Then she turned, almost tripping over Sierra, to head back downstairs to the rec room.

Rather than going all the way down, though, she lowered herself to the floor, positioning herself so she was in front of the door.

Sierra made a circle, then sat right next to her, facing outward, her ears perked forward.

"Good girl, Sierra." Talking to the dog helped calm her

frayed nerves. She swallowed hard and rested the gun in her lap, holding it in both hands.

It wouldn't be easy to fire at the dark-haired man, the way she'd shredded a paper target. But she would do whatever was necessary if he made it this far.

*Please, Lord, please don't let him get inside the house!*

# CHAPTER TEN

For a moment, Kaleb felt like he was back in the Afghan desert as he crept along the side of the house. Images of Afghan soldiers popping out from behind dwellings and shooting indiscriminately flashed in his mind. He shook off the memory, unwilling to allow the past to distract him.

He listened intently but only heard the occasional car engine chugging by. There was very little speeding along the residential streets of this neighborhood.

Then he heard leaves rustling. Had the dark-haired guy fallen into one of his traps? He prayed that he'd finally get his hands on this guy. More thudding sounds spurred Kaleb to quicken his pace.

Off to the right, a flash of movement caught his eye. Jumping over one of the trip wires, Kaleb tried to catch up. But just like the night before, the guy somehow managed to disappear out of sight. Still, how far could he have gone? Kaleb moved onto the neighbor's property, searching for evidence the guy had been there.

There was an indentation of a footprint in the ground near some decorative shrubs. He made a mental note to take a picture later for evidence as he continued moving forward.

He went through yet another neighbor's backyard before he heard the sound of a car engine. Sprinting across the terrain, he reached the road just in time to see the tail-lights of a black truck disappearing around the corner. The license plate had been covered with mud, so he felt certain the driver had been the intruder they were searching for.

Kaleb rubbed his right knee for a minute, then turned back. He retraced his steps slowly, hoping to find more evidence. But he didn't find anything else by the time he ended up back at the footprint next to the shrubbery.

After taking several photos, using his own foot as a reference, he went back to check on his trip wires. It didn't take long for him to find that the wire closest to the edge of the property had been snapped.

The guy had gone down, but he still managed to get away.

The wire had protected them, but he'd really hoped the guy would come toward the trio of palm trees. If he'd have done that, the net might have held him up long enough for Kaleb to get there.

He took a moment to check the rest of his trip wires. All were good. He debated whether or not to replace the one the guy had snapped. Leaving it broken might encourage the man to keep going all the way to the trio of palm trees where he had the net suspended.

Then again, the trip wire had put the guy on notice. Would he be doubly careful next time? Very likely, at least in searching for more trip wires, but maybe not in looking up over his head. Kaleb decided to leave everything as it was. He stood near the corner of the property and called Grimes.

"Now what?" The detective sounded more tired than annoyed.

"I chased off another intruder out here. I'm sending you a picture of a footprint I found." As he spoke, he sent the photographs. "Figured this might come in handy when you get your hands on Thomas Acker."

"Where was this found?" Grimes asked.

"Near some decorative shrubs in the yard next door. Hold on, I know what you're going to say," Kaleb interrupted. "Yes, it could belong to anyone, including the property owners or a hired landscaper. I get that, but you have to admit it would be a giant coincidence if this print is the same size and has the same tread as Thomas Acker's."

Grimes made a grunting noise that Kaleb decided to take as agreement. Then he asked, "You didn't see him?"

"Only his back after he took off running. I set up trip wires, which stopped him from getting too close."

"Trip wires?" Surprise echoed from Grimes's tone.

"Yeah. Unfortunately, it didn't work as well as I'd hoped. He ran through several neighbors' yards, then escaped in a black truck with mud-smeared license plates." He paused, then added, "It may be time to bring in the local police."

"I'm happy to make the call as soon as you tell me which jurisdiction you're located within."

He holstered his weapon, moved around the corner of the house, stepped over his trip line, and went up the steps. "Give me some time to talk to Charlotte about that."

"All right, I'll wait to hear back from you," Grimes said. "Good work on keeping them safe, Tyson."

Kaleb didn't respond because a failed mission was not something to celebrate. Yes, Charlotte and the others were safe, but they were still being actively stalked by this dark-haired guy.

And so far, he and Grimes were no closer to catching him.

After keying in the code, he stepped inside the house and activated the alarm. "Charlotte? It's safe to come out. Everything is fine."

Charlotte stepped out into the great room, coming from the door that led down to the rec room. He grimaced when he saw the gun in her hand. "He got away?"

"I'm afraid so. He broke through a trip wire, and that scared him off. He had a truck parked on another street. I saw his black truck, but mud covered the license plates, making it impossible to get the number."

She gave a curt nod. "Nice to know your trip wires worked."

"Yeah." He gestured to her gun. "I'm sorry you were scared enough to grab that."

"No way was I going to allow him to get past me." She grimaced. "I need to put this away before any of the kids see it, especially Tommy."

"Charlotte." He crossed the room to pull her into his arms. "You are the strongest, bravest woman I know."

She rested against him for a long minute before pulling back far enough to gaze up at him. "I'm not. Don't you remember what I told you? I ran away from Jerry like a coward rather than standing up to him."

He frowned. "Taking care of yourself is not cowardly. You needed time to regroup. To get back on your feet. I admire you for what you've accomplished here."

His heart wept at the uncertainty in her gaze. "You don't think I should have stayed in Minneapolis to press charges?"

"I may have felt that way once, but not anymore. Not when I see what you and the other women are facing every day. Now I blame our flawed legal system, one in which a guy can do something so awful as abusing a woman and child yet be out on bail in a matter of hours."

"That certainly doesn't help," Charlotte agreed.

He slowly drew her closer. "You are an amazing woman, Charlotte Cambridge."

A reluctant smile tipped at the corner of her mouth. "Thank you," she murmured. Then she rose onto her tiptoes and kissed him. In some part of his mind, he knew the gesture stemmed from simple gratitude, but that didn't stop him from drawing her close, savoring her sweet kiss, relishing every moment of their embrace.

His world felt stable when he had Charlotte in his arms. He did his best to keep his desire in check, slowly easing back on the kiss until they were both able to breathe again.

"Don't you dare apologize." Charlotte's voice was muffled against his chest.

He grinned, smoothing a hand down her back. "I won't. As much as I'd rather stay here kissing you, we should probably tell the others they're safe now."

Her eyes widened. "Oh, yes. How could I forget?" She stepped away from him, looking flustered. "Ah, you do that while I put the gun away."

He'd be lying if he didn't admit how much he enjoyed making her forget where she was or what she was doing. Kaleb pulled himself together and opened the door to the rec room. "Milly? It's Kaleb coming down."

"Kaleb!" several of the women called his name in obvious relief.

He quickly joined them, raking his gaze over the group

huddled together on the large sectional sofa. "Everyone is safe, there's no threat."

Willow stared at him for a long moment before kissing the top of Tommy's head. "Thank you."

The reality of the grim situation weighed heavily on his shoulders. Not only had he failed to apprehend this guy, but he'd also failed in his goal to provide a safe place for the women and children looking back at him.

He desperately wanted to go on offense, the way the Navy SEALs had approached every single one of their ops.

But he couldn't leave them alone either. Not to mention, he had little to no intel to go on.

Should he call Mason Gray, his former team leader? San Diego was a solid four to five hours from here, but he knew their Senior Chief wouldn't hesitate to hit the road first thing.

Then again, adding another strange man to the mix might be pushing things with the women and children who were huddling together in fear already.

He needed to discuss their next steps with Charlotte. He offered the group another smile. "Keep watching your movies. Charlotte and I need to chat with the detective on the case."

"I need to prepare lunch," Milly announced.

They'd only finished breakfast ninety minutes ago, but he understood Milly took her role of feeding the group seriously. "Sure thing."

He followed Milly upstairs. When he saw Charlotte coming down the grand staircase, his heart squeezed in his chest. Keeping her at a safe distance was a losing battle. Still, he forced himself to concentrate on their next steps.

"Charlotte?" He gestured toward the study. "We need to talk."

She joined him in the room, her gaze going to the window that overlooked the spot where the dark-haired guy had been. Then she turned to face him. "We should let Grimes know what happened."

"I did that, but the bigger question here is whether or not we put the local police on notice."

She grimaced. "Only if we're planning to stay. I think it's obvious we should relocate again."

"We can certainly do that, but only if the new place has some of the same amenities we have here, like the security system and the recreational room." He wasn't keen on all the windows, but all private homes in this area would have the same set up. "The trip wires I set up worked in that they prevented him from getting close."

"Yeah, but now he knows to look for them, right?"

"Yes, but I highly doubt he'd find them all." He hesitated, then added, "We may want to give Grimes time to get Thomas Acker in custody. Adding the local police in this area would help in that respect."

She sighed and rubbed her temples. "I honestly don't know what to do, Kaleb. Normally we would relocate, but clearly having a bus show up here to get all the women and children out would be noticeable, especially in this neighborhood. What if the dark-haired guy is positioned somewhere nearby, watching for us to do exactly that?"

He'd had the same thought. "If he is hiding somewhere nearby, I'll find him. I just need to get one of my former teammates here to keep an eye on the house." He hesitated, then added, "No one is close, though. Which is why I keep going back to the idea of getting the local police involved. For all we know, one of the neighbors has already filed a report about seeing a trespasser."

"Okay, let's do it." She drew in a deep breath. "And if

you want to head out to look for him, I can stay here alone. We managed while you were outside earlier. Having an alarm system helps. We can stay down in the rec room while you're gone."

He hated the idea of leaving them here, yet he also knew Charlotte was used to manning a safe house alone. She was armed and knew how to use a gun.

Yet he still didn't like putting her in that position.

"Let's call Grimes first." He pulled out his phone.

The detective answered on the first ring. "Tyson? Everyone okay?"

"We're fine," Kaleb reassured him. "Any news on Acker?"

"Not yet. What did you and Charlotte decide?"

"I'm here, Detective," Charlotte said, her gaze locked on Kaleb's. "We've decided to let you call the locals. We're hoping someone may have seen this guy slinking around."

"I know this wasn't an easy decision," Grimes said.

Kaleb rattled off the address. "If you could give the local detective my number, I'd appreciate it."

"Will do."

"One more thing, Detective," Charlotte said. "Will you be on alert for Emma Yonkers? She left the safe house here yesterday, and well, I'm worried about her."

"Not much I can do about that," Grimes pointed out. "You don't think she'll go back to the guy who hurt her, do you?"

"Maybe. His name is Rodney Jones. And I know there isn't much you can do, but I guess I'm hoping if a call comes through about her, the officers will take it seriously."

"We take all abuse calls seriously, but I get what you're saying." Grimes paused, then added, "I'll call Agoura Hills right now."

"Thanks." Kaleb pushed the end button on the screen and slipped the phone into his pocket. "I know you're worried about Emma, but the Los Angeles police department is huge. It's not likely Grimes will be able to do much."

"I know." She shrugged. "It was her choice to leave, but that doesn't mean I won't worry about her."

He nodded, understanding exactly where she was coming from. Didn't he have concerns about Hudson? He lightly rested his hand on her arm. "I won't leave until we hear back from the Agoura Hills police department."

"Okay." She wrapped her arms around her waist. "I hope we're doing the right thing, Kaleb."

*Yeah*, he thought grimly, *me too*.

---

GIVING Detective Grimes their safe house location wasn't as difficult as she'd anticipated. Keeping secrets had been second nature over the last four years. Yet she'd learned to trust Kaleb's instincts over these past few days.

She hoped he was right about the neighbors potentially reporting him as a trespasser or peeping Tom. It would force the Agoura Hills police department to take this threat seriously.

Kaleb was right, though, about the size of the Los Angeles Police Department. Why had she mentioned Emma? Normally, she didn't ruminate over the women who decided to leave her safe house. She'd long ago learned to focus on saving those who wanted to be saved.

Like Willow and Tommy. Along with the others currently staying with her.

"We'll pray for her." Kaleb came up to stand beside her.

"How did you know I was thinking of Emma?"

"You looked sad." Kaleb reached out to take her hand. "And I know you asked Grimes about her because you're worried."

"I am, yes. She's young and foolish enough to go back to her abuser." She looked down at their joined hands. "I think praying is a good thing to do."

"Dear Lord, we ask You to keep Emma Yonkers safe in Your loving care. Guide her to safety. Amen."

"Amen." She managed a smile. "Thanks, Kaleb. I—uh, should go see if Milly needs help."

"Good idea." He squeezed her hand, then released her. "I'll be in shortly."

"Okay." She forced herself to walk away from him rather than throw herself into his arms. Kaleb was messing with her head, making her want things she couldn't have.

Running a safe house was her life. Her mission. She'd chosen to do this work, and that meant there was no room for a relationship.

The sooner she accepted that reality, the better.

Milly didn't need help, so she went down into the rec room to check on the residents. She stayed with them, enjoying the Disney movie they'd been watching. After an hour, the movie ended.

"There may be time to watch another one," she told them.

"Why can't we go swimming?" Tommy asked.

"It's chilly outside today," she informed him. "The high temp is only sixty-four degrees, and that's too cold to be out in the pool."

"I thought you said we had to stay inside to be safe?" Tommy challenged.

"That too. But it's also too cold." She caught Willow's

gaze. "You can stay down here to watch another show, or you can head back upstairs." She glanced at her watch. "Milly will have lunch ready in about an hour."

"I think we should stay down here," Willow said. The other women murmured in agreement.

Charlotte hated knowing how afraid Willow was at the possibility that Tommy's father had come to find them. She wouldn't be surprised if Willow and Tommy decided to sleep in the recreation room that night.

It wasn't a half-bad idea.

Charlotte left them to their movie, heading back upstairs. She followed the sound of Kaleb's voice to the den. "Yes, sir. I served in the navy for twenty-two years."

Who was he talking to? She caught his gaze and lifted a brow.

"I appreciate you following up on the conversation you had with Detective Grimes." Kaleb gestured for her to come closer, then put the call on speaker. "Have you had any calls about suspicious men moving around the neighborhood?"

"No, but we did have a call about a young woman who appeared to be a prostitute," the male voice said. "She was gone by the time officers arrived to talk to her."

*Not a prostitute*, Charlotte thought with a sigh. She mouthed the word Emma to Kaleb who nodded.

"That may have been Emma Yonkers," Kaleb said. "She was one of the safe house residents, before she decided to leave yesterday. She was dressed in rather tight clothing, but I can assure you, she's not a prostitute."

"Emma Yonkers, huh? Okay, I'll make a note that she should not be treated as a prostitution suspect."

"Detective Wales, I'm more interested in anyone who reports seeing a guy hanging around," Kaleb said. "I chased someone off the property twice in a matter of hours. Someone must have noticed."

"I'll go through the intake calls again," the detective offered. "Narrowing in on the area immediately around your location."

Her stomach knotted a bit at that. She told herself to get over it.

"Thanks," Kaleb said. "I also saw a black truck with muddied license plates."

"That's illegal, and our guys would pick up on something like that," Detective Wales said. "I'll put out notice for our officers to be aware of that too."

"Okay." Kaleb lifted a brow, silently asking if there was anything she wanted to add. She shook her head. "Thanks again, we appreciate everything you're doing to keep the women and children here safe."

"Not a problem. We'll find this guy." It almost sounded as if the detective relished the task at hand.

Kaleb disconnected. "I think we made the right decision, Charlotte. This isn't a high crime area like Los Angeles. The Agoura Hills police will be far more likely to pull over someone who doesn't look as if they belong."

"No kidding. I can't believe someone assumed Emma was a prostitute."

"It's just that she doesn't fit in around here, right? She wouldn't draw a second glance in downtown Los Angeles." He shrugged. "Personally, I'm glad she left before she could get arrested. I'm sure that accusation would not have gone over very well with her. Hopefully she found a taxi or a bus."

She eyed him curiously. "You gave her money, didn't you?"

He flushed. "Hey, I just wanted to make sure she had a

way to get back to Los Angeles. I was afraid she'd accept a ride from a stranger, which would not be good."

"You're a softie," she chided, although she was secretly relived that he'd been concerned enough to help her out. "Emma knows how to take care of herself. She grew up in foster care, which is how she ended up with a lowlife like Rodney in the first place."

"I'm sure she can take care of herself as long as she makes smart choices." He stood and gestured toward the great room. "I'm going to head out to see if our suspect is hiding out nearby."

"Now? Why not wait until after lunch?"

"I thought you said you'd be okay being here alone with the alarm system on?" he asked with concern.

"I am, but Milly takes pride in feeding you." Maybe she was a little afraid, but there was no sense in mentioning that. Up until a few days ago, she'd never had a man like Kaleb watching over her. Especially not a former Navy SEAL with enough knowledge to set up trip wires around the property.

Time for her to grow a backbone. She never should have allowed herself to become dependent on Kaleb's protection in the first place.

Although she'd never had a former abuser come to shoot at her safe house either.

"Lunch is almost ready," Milly called from the kitchen. "Char, will you call the women and children up from the rec room?"

"Yes, of course." She turned away, wondering if Willow would feel safe enough to return to the main level.

Kaleb's phone rang. He put a hand on her arm to stop her. "It's Detective Grimes."

"Let's go back into the study." It wasn't that she didn't

trust Milly, but she wanted to protect the woman and the others from potential bad news.

"Tyson," Kaleb answered curtly, automatically putting the call on speaker for her benefit. "What's going on, Detective?"

"Is Charlotte Cambridge nearby?"

"I'm here," she answered, her stomach knotting with fear. "Sounds like you have bad news, Detective."

"I need to show you a picture of a homicide victim that was found early this morning." He didn't beat around the bush.

"Send it to me," Kaleb said.

She frowned. "Send it to both of us," she corrected. "It sounds as if you believe this victim is one of my former safe house residents?"

"Unfortunately, yes. There was no ID found on her, and her prints are not in the system." Grimes took a moment, then said, "I sent the photos."

She stared at her phone until the text message popped up on the screen. When she saw Emma's battered face, she bit back a cry, a wave of grief pummeling her.

The flirty young woman was dead.

# CHAPTER ELEVEN

"That is Emma Yonkers," Kaleb said grimly. He wrapped his arm around Charlotte's waist, fearing she'd collapse at the news of Emma's murder. "As we mentioned last night, she was one of our safe house residents."

"Yeah? Any idea how she ended up lying in the alley near the old safe house location?" Grimes asked.

"She left the safe house here in Agoura Hills yesterday." Kaleb wished he'd tried harder to convince Emma to stay with them. "I gave her money for a taxi or rideshare."

"You need to find Rodney Jones," Charlotte said, her voice thick with emotion. "He's her former boyfriend. He abused her in the past."

"Charlotte is right. Emma told me she didn't think Rodney was a bad guy, that he was sorry for what he'd done. I believe she probably went back to him."

"I'll get a BOLO issued for him ASAP," Grimes said. "Although you should know that we don't believe she was murdered where her body was found."

Charlotte let out a choked sound. "You mean, someone may have killed her here in Agoura Hills?"

"I don't know where she was murdered," Grimes quickly said. "We need to cover all possibilities."

"Maybe the crime scene is Rodney's apartment, or somewhere close to where he lives," Kaleb said, his mind whirling with different theories of the crime. Had Rodney killed Emma, dumping her body near the safe house as a not so subtle message? As in, don't even bother to try to keep women safe? A chilling thought. "Is Rodney Jones in the system? Was he included in the mug shots you showed Charlotte?"

"Just a minute." Grimes was silent for a moment, then said, "Yeah, he's in the system. For drugs, not for assault and battery. I'll send you a copy of his mug shot."

Charlotte leaned against him as they waited for her phone to ping. The picture was of a dark-skinned man. He had dark hair, but the facial features were different. It was difficult to say for certain, but he didn't think Rodney was the guy he'd seen outside the safe house.

"I don't think that's him," Charlotte said, her tone anything but certain. "I think the man following me was more pale, as if he didn't get out in the sun much. And Rodney's eyes are closer together than what I remember."

"I agree with Charlotte, but I do think it's possible he killed Emma." Kaleb tried to push aside the dark despair. He felt terrible that young Emma had been brutally murdered. He'd hoped her killer was the same one who was trying to get inside the safe house.

Unfortunately, not. That would have been too easy.

And every SEAL knew the only easy day was yesterday.

"What time did she leave your safe house?" Grimes asked.

Kaleb gave him the pertinent information. "The Agoura

Hills detective, a guy named Wales, mentioned someone complained about Emma, the caller assumed she was a prostitute. Call him to find out what time that call came in. That may help your timeline."

"I will." There was a pause before Grimes said, "Any update on your perp?"

"No." He didn't feel the need to explain how he was going to head out to hunt for him. "I gave Detective Wales the information, he promised to keep an eye out for him."

"Okay, thanks for the information on Ms. Yonkers," Grimes said.

"Please keep me updated on what you find out," Charlotte said. "Emma may have left the safe house by her choice, but she didn't deserve to die."

"I agree. Take care." Grimes disconnected from the call.

Charlotte pushed away from Kaleb, running her fingers through her short hair. "I can't believe she's dead."

"Maybe we keep this news to ourselves for a bit," Kaleb suggested. "No reason to upset everyone."

"We can tell them later," Charlotte agreed. "But honestly, they should know what happened. If Emma hadn't left us, she'd still be alive. That's the hard truth about abuse and the most difficult for victims to understand. They always think it can't happen to them, but the number of abused women who die or are permanently disabled is staggering." She shook her head sadly. "I can save many of these women and children, but I can't save them all."

"You do great work, Charlotte. Stay focused on the ones you have saved. As you said, this isn't a jail. Everyone has to make their own choices and be responsible for the consequences." Kaleb hadn't really understood the impact of what she'd accomplished until now. When Emma left, she truly felt she'd be fine. Until she wasn't. "Let's wait until after lunch at least."

She nodded and walked out of the office. He followed, wishing there was something he could say or do to make her feel better. He sent up a silent prayer that God would bring Emma home.

Milly frowned, picking up on their grim mood. But she didn't say anything as she served the chili she'd made for lunch. When they were all seated, Milly and Charlotte looked at him expectantly.

He folded his hands and bowed his head. "Dear Lord, please bless this food You've provided for us. Also continue to keep us all safe in Your care and protect us from those who wish to do us harm. Amen."

"Amen," Milly, Charlotte, and several others echoed.

The chili tasted great, but it was hard to enjoy the meal with Emma's murder hanging over him. He eyed Charlotte, noticing how she picked at her food too. When he'd finished eating, he carried his dishes to the sink. Charlotte quickly joined him.

"Are you leaving soon?" she asked in a low voice.

"Yes. I need to find this guy." He flashed a reassuring smile. "You and the residents will be fine. The security system is engaged, and if you hear anything outside, call 911. In this neighborhood, the response should be swift. And I have enough trip wires to keep him from getting too close."

"I will." Her attempt at a smile was pathetic. "Be safe, Kaleb."

"You too." He couldn't help himself from pressing a quick kiss to the top of her head, filling his senses with her unique fragrance. Then he turned to Sierra. "Stay. Guard."

Sierra sat, although her dark eyes seemed to beg him to

take her along with him. Tempting, but he felt certain having the dog with him would only attract more attention as he attempted to stealthily move around the neighborhood.

Leaving Charlotte wasn't easy. But sitting around and waiting for this guy to make another move would be worse. Going on offense seemed to be the best solution. And hopefully one that this guy wouldn't expect.

"Activate the alarm when I leave," he said to Charlotte.

"I will." He left the house, moving around the perimeter to make sure the assailant wasn't hiding nearby.

Kaleb took his time, his gaze alert as he silently moved from one spot to the next. He took note of the neighboring properties, identifying all potential hiding spots.

His SEAL training had instilled the value of patience. Some things couldn't be rushed, and he wasn't about to tip this guy off. Yet California didn't provide a lot of cover either. A few scrubby bushes, tall, slender palm trees, and houses and garages were all he had to work with.

Yet those were the same limitations the dark-haired guy had to deal with too. And Kaleb had faith in his superior training and skills.

And in God watching over him.

As he edged around the property directly behind their current safe house, he raked his gaze over the ridge off to the right. Agoura Hills was aptly named; several houses were tucked up against a ridge. He understood the desire of homeowners to build high along the ridge in hopes of capturing a glimpse of the ocean.

The rocky terrain offered additional hiding spots. It reminded him of Afghanistan, where the Taliban fighters would lie in wait before jumping out from behind a rock, shooting indiscriminately.

It took him an hour to clear the ridge. He didn't find a footprint similar to the one he'd photographed earlier. Maybe he was giving this guy too much credit; thus far, he hadn't really gotten his hands dirty, sticking mostly with firing his weapon. Kaleb made his way back to the safe house, taking several minutes to assess whether anyone had been there.

His trip wires were intact, so he decided to keep moving. The only area he hadn't checked out was along the street itself. To him, that wasn't a good place to hide. Yet on the other hand, if this guy didn't have military training, he may have taken the easy way in and out.

There were some vehicles parked on the road, but none were black trucks with mud-smeared license plates. The smaller house located directly across the street appeared quiet; there were no cars in the driveway. He continued searching the main street, then made his way down each of the side streets.

He slowed his pace when he saw a black truck parked on the side of the road. The front end was facing him, and he could easily read the license plate. The first letter an H, not an A or a 4. Still, he quickly memorized it, then cautiously approached the vehicle.

No one was inside. He moved around to the back, frowning when he noticed the license plate. It matched the front plate and wasn't covered in mud.

He kept walking until he reached the end of the cul-de-sac without seeing anyone wandering around nearby. Not even occupants of the various houses, which seemed a bit unusual, although to most people living here, it was too cold to do anything outside. Turning, he retraced his steps, going once more past the black truck.

A coincidence? There had to be dozens of black

trucks in Agoura Hills. Yet he wasn't about to ignore the possible lead. He pulled out his phone to call Detective Wales. The guy didn't pick up, so he left a message. "This is Kaleb Tyson, we spoke earlier today about a man lurking around our safe house. I'd like you to run the following license plate through the system." He rattled off the information. "I'd like to know who the vehicle is registered to and where he or she lives. I'm standing on Hillside Court. Please call me back with what you find out, thanks."

There wasn't much more he could do about this vehicle, so he continued surveilling additional side streets. Another hour later, he returned to Paradise Drive, the street upon which the safe house was located. He blew out a frustrated breath at coming up empty-handed.

No sign of the dark-haired guy or a truck with muddy license plates.

He hadn't heard back from Wales either. He pulled out his phone to call the detective again as he walked briskly down the side street where he'd seen the truck. Then he stopped abruptly.

It was gone.

He frowned, examining the houses nearby. The most likely explanation was that the truck was owned by one of the residents living there. Someone who left to go to work, or to the gym, or the grocery store.

"Wales," the detective answered.

"This is Kaleb Tyson. I'm following up on the message I left you earlier." He was about to add that the information was likely a false alarm when the detective surprised him.

"I was just about to call you, Tyson. The license plate you identified is registered to a man who lives in Los Angeles. He drives a dark green truck, not a black one."

Kaleb tightened his grip on the phone. "Are you telling me the truck was stolen?"

"I'm waiting to hear back from Darrin McCoy, but yeah, that's my take on it. Any chance you took down the VIN number?"

"No." He mentally kicked himself for not thinking of that. He was proving to be a lousy investigator. Then again, he'd never worked as a cop. "And even worse, the truck is gone."

"That's interesting. Do you think someone saw you checking it out?"

"He must have." Kaleb slowly turned in a circle, wondering where the guy had been hiding. The front lawns didn't offer any coverage, and hiding up near a house in broad daylight was risky. But that must have been what the perp had done. "I didn't see him, though."

"Don't worry, we'll find it," Wales said with confidence. "My guess is that this guy swapped license plates with the green truck. Then he smeared mud across the surface to avoid being caught right away. It's a tactic other auto thieves have used before. Especially if their intent is to use the vehicle to commit a crime."

"Yeah." He swept his gaze up and down the street. "The odd thing is that he took the time to remove the mud from the rear plate. I hate to admit, that caught me off guard. Let me know what Darrin McCoy from LA says." He hesitated, then added, "This is on me. I should have stayed near the truck to catch this guy."

"The truck could have belonged to anyone," Wales pointed out. "Besides, we'll find him."

Kaleb ended the call, wishing he could believe that. Unfortunately, it seemed as if he'd let their best lead slip away.

And he had no one to blame but himself.

―――――――

"WHAT'S WRONG?" Milly demanded. "Are you that worried about Kaleb? He's clearly a man capable of taking care of himself."

"Yes, no, I mean . . ." Charlotte sighed. "I learned some disturbing news earlier."

Milly's eyes widened. "What?"

She hesitated, then reminded herself that Milly deserved to know. "Emma's body was found near our old safe house. She was murdered."

Milly sucked in a harsh breath, then crossed herself. "Dear Lord, please have mercy on Emma's soul," she whispered.

"Yes." Oddly, the housekeeper's prayer made her feel slightly better. "I'm sure she ended up going back to her abuser, only to pay the ultimate price."

"That's not your fault, Char," Milly said, reaching out to touch her arm. "You warned Emma, and I know Kaleb did too. We can't control the decisions these women make. All we can do is guide them the best we can."

"I know. But maybe I should have tried harder with Emma." Charlotte winced as she thought back to how she'd told Emma to stay away from Kaleb, a man old enough to be her father. "I was too hard on her."

"She was the one who flirted with Kaleb, as if he would be interested in a young woman like her," Milly retorted.

"I know. But she was so young, so impressionable, maybe if I'd have let her down gently—"

"You always tell the women who come here not to play the what-if game," Milly said briskly. "Time to take your own advice. We both sensed Emma wasn't satisfied with the strict rules. She would have left sooner or later."

"Maybe." Charlotte tried to shake off the guilt. "It just hurts to know how much she suffered."

"Everyone here has suffered." Milly pierced her with a stern gaze. "Including you."

Charlotte nodded, knowing Milly was right. "I'm at a loss as to what to tell the others."

The older woman grimaced. "Do you have to tell them anything?"

Truthfully, she didn't want to. But she nodded. "They deserve to know the danger. Besides, if there's any chance this will help them stay away from their own abusers, I have to take it."

"It could also make them that much more fearful," Milly muttered. "Willow is already jumping at the slightest noise."

"I know, and I don't necessarily want to tell the kids either. They don't need to hear this." Charlotte thought for a moment. "Would you mind going down to the rec room? Send the women up here while you watch the kids."

"Of course." Milly hurried off.

The women filed into the dining room, looking at her with apprehension.

"Are we moving again?" Willow asked.

"Not yet." She'd agreed to wait and see what Kaleb found. "But I'm afraid I have distressing news about Emma."

"She in the hospital?" Janet asked.

"No. Unfortunately, she's been murdered."

Willow gasped, then clamped her hands over her mouth. A murmur rose among the others.

"I wasn't going to tell you," Charlotte said. "But there's

a strong possibility Emma went back to her abuser. You need to understand that violence against women is wrong and should never be tolerated. And going back to the same abusive partner is asking for trouble."

"She was so young," Jodie whispered.

"I can't believe it," Kim whispered.

"I know, it's heartbreaking." Charlotte sighed. "Just stick with the rules, okay? And even if you decide to leave, please don't go back to your abuser."

"Or go anyplace he might find you," Willow added. Her face was void of all color, and Charlotte knew she was thinking about her ex-husband and the pain he'd inflicted upon her and Tommy.

"Exactly. That's why we have a relocation program." Charlotte took solace in the fact that these women wouldn't make the same mistake Emma had. It offered some solace, especially those with children. "Please know that Kaleb and I are doing everything possible to keep you safe from harm."

The women looked at each other, and it was sad to see the shadow of doubt darken their gazes.

After the residents returned downstairs, Charlotte moved from window to window with her gun hidden beneath the hem of her sweater. It was bulky and felt unnatural, but she forced herself to ignore the discomfort.

The dark clouds swirling outside only reinforced her despondent mood. She found herself praying God would guide Kaleb and the police to the dark-haired man. That he be brought to justice very soon so they could return to their previous safe house.

This time, though, the prayer didn't make her feel better. She wondered if God was really watching over them. He hadn't protected Emma.

What was it that Kaleb had said? Explaining about how

God had a plan for them? Did that mean His plan for Emma included her dying at the hands of her abuser?

If so, why?

Charlotte dragged in a deep breath, struggling to maintain her composure. If Kaleb was here, he'd tell her it wasn't up to them to question God's plan. But that was far easier said than done.

She heard a sound coming from the front door. Hurrying over, she relaxed when she saw Kaleb enter.

"What's wrong?" he asked the moment he saw her expression. He quickly crossed over to her.

She shook her head, trying not to cry. "Nothing really. It was just more difficult telling the residents about Emma than I anticipated. I mean, normally we don't hear anything about the women after they leave us."

"You should have waited for me to get back." His gaze was full of concern as he pulled her into his arms. "I'm sorry you had to go through that."

She leaned against him, absorbing his strength. It was becoming a habit for her, one she needed to break and soon. But for now, she relished being held in Kaleb's warm embrace.

After a few seconds, she lifted her head. "Did you find anything?"

He grimaced and turned back to activate the alarm. "I messed up. I found a black truck parked on a side street, no mud on the license plates, so I didn't really think it was the one we were looking for. Plus, I didn't see anyone inside, and there weren't hiding spots nearby. Just to be on the safe side, I left a message with Detective Wales. When he called me back, he confirmed the truck was likely stolen, the plates belonged to a dark green truck owned by someone in Los Angeles, not a black one. I think it must have been used by our dark-haired guy. But by the time I got back there, the truck was gone."

She empathized with his disappointment but tried to look on the bright side. Ironically, Kaleb's deep regret made her long to cheer him up. "You probably scared him off, Kaleb, which could be a good thing. Maybe he'll give up and leave for good."

"We can't assume that. In fact, he could be feeling pretty smug about getting away. I should have done better," Kaleb said grimly. "If I had stayed nearby or canvassed the area better, I'd have found him."

"Don't take responsibility for his actions," she said. "That's what you told me, remember?"

"I'm taking responsibility for my own actions," he corrected. "The failure is mine. But there's nothing I can do to change that now. Hopefully, Detective Wales will find the stolen vehicle."

Personally, she had more faith in Kaleb than in either detective. Not that they weren't trying, but Kaleb was the one who had obtained each lead in the case so far. "Everything has been quiet here," she informed him.

"I was hoping that was the case," he admitted. "I double-checked that my trip wires and net trap were still intact, but I won't underestimate this guy again. He may have realized I have several more trip wires hidden."

"I doubt he's as smart as you, Kaleb."

A hint of a smile tugged at the corner of his mouth. "Thanks for the vote of confidence, but we know he's been smart enough to elude capture this long."

"You mentioned before this is all part of God's plan," Charlotte said. "You really believe that?"

"I do. There's a quote from Proverbs three, verses five to six: 'Trust in the Lord with all your heart and lean not on your own understanding: in all your ways acknowledge him, and he will keep your path straight.'"

She nodded thoughtfully. "I like that."

"Tommy! Where are you?"

Willow's voice had them both turning toward the stairway leading up from the rec room. "What's wrong?" Charlotte asked.

"Tommy's missing." Willow's eyes were wide with fear. "I—he was watching *Mulan* with the other kids, and now he's not there. Did you see him come upstairs?"

"No, but the alarm would have sounded if he'd tried to leave the house," Charlotte reminded her. "I'm sure he's here somewhere."

"Tommy? Come here right now!" Willow called sharply.

"Check your bedroom," Kaleb suggested. "We'll spread out and search."

Willow bolted up the grand staircase.

"I'll take the study," Kaleb said. "You check the kitchen and dining room."

"Tommy?" she called for the boy, searching possible hiding places. "You're not in trouble, Tommy. We only want to know you're safe."

There was no answer. A sliver of icy fear slipped down her spine. There was no way the child could have escaped. Not without setting off the alarm.

Then she remembered the brief moments she'd clung to Kaleb before he'd turned back to activate the alarm. Was it possible Tommy had managed to open a window and go outside at that exact moment? Highly unlikely.

Yet the thought nagged at her as they continued searching the house.

"Tommy! Please come out," Willow begged.

Charlotte went down to the recreation room to find the other three kids. Tommy was the oldest, but that didn't mean they hadn't seen something.

She knelt on the floor beside Rachel, Angela, and Tonya. "Did you see where Tommy went?"

"No." Rachel shook her head while Angela stuck her thumb in her mouth.

"Is he hiding?" Tonya asked.

"Maybe, but no one else is playing hide-and-seek, right?"

The three kids shook their heads.

"I wanna watch *Mulan*," Angela said, her words muffled by her thumb.

"Me too," Tonya added as Rachel nodded vigorously.

She rose and glanced around the room. Next to the rec room there was a storage space. She expected it to be dark, but there was some light coming in from a small basement window.

Hurrying over, she examined the window. Thankfully, the window was connected to the alarm system.

The rest of the women were searching now too. As much as she tried to think logically, she couldn't help feeling panicked. This couldn't really be God's plan, could it?

First Emma's murder, now this?

Where was Tommy?

## CHAPTER TWELVE

Kaleb didn't think Tommy could have gotten out in the narrow time frame the alarm wasn't activated, but he still felt guilty for allowing that much of a delay in resetting it.

His fault for allowing himself to be distracted by Charlotte's distress. He'd gone straight to comfort her rather than covering his six.

Unacceptable.

"He's not in our room," Willow said, coming down the grand staircase. "I don't understand. Where he could be?"

"We'll find him." Kaleb injected as much confidence as possible into his tone. He glanced toward the second floor. It occurred to him that the windows on that level were not connected to the alarm system. It was understandable, really. The cost of adding sensor alarms to all of those windows would be a waste of time and money since it wasn't likely that a robber would bring a ladder to break into the place.

Charlotte came up from the rec room. "The kids think he might be playing hide-and-seek."

He nodded, but it seemed strange. Why bother to hide

if no one was going to come and find you? "I need to check a few things upstairs."

Willow and Charlotte followed him up. He almost told them to wait downstairs, then realized that wasn't fair. Willow was desperate to find her son, and shutting her out of the possibility rolling through his mind wouldn't be the best answer.

If he found Tommy, he'd need her help.

Working methodically, he moved from one room to the next, starting in the master suite that Charlotte and Milly shared. The windows were shut and locked, no sign of Tommy being inside.

The room he and Willow shared was next, but there, too, the window was locked and closed. He hesitated, though, noticing how a portion of the roof line jutted out, seemingly over the study. After mentally reviewing the floor plan, he turned and went to the next room over, one that was used by Jodie and her daughter, Angela.

Upon entering the room, his stomach knotted and clenched when he saw the open window. He hurried over and lifted the frame as high as it could go. The knot in his stomach tightened when he saw the boy sitting out along the edge of the slanted roof.

"Hey, Tommy." Kaleb kept his tone casual as he threw one leg over the bottom edge of the opening. "What are you doing?"

"I wanna go home." Tommy's voice hitched, and his face was streaked with tears.

"I understand you're upset, but why did you come out here?" Folding his large frame to get through the window opening wasn't easy. Behind him, he heard Willow gasp in horror and prayed she wouldn't scare Tommy by yelling at the kid. If he was startled, he could slip off the roof. "It's not safe for you to be out here, Tommy. What if you fell?"

"I don't care." The boy's tone was defiant. "I wanna go home. I'm sick of playing with Angela, Rachel, and Tonya. They're just girls." He said the last word as if they were green aliens rather than a couple of kids not much younger than him.

Kaleb slowly edged closer. "Hey, I understand what it's like to miss hanging out with your friends. A few of my friends live in a completely different state."

Tommy swiped at his face. "Does your mom let you visit them? Because mine won't."

He slid a little closer. Another couple of feet and he'd be within reach to grab the child if he lost his balance. "My friends are too far away that I can't really visit them. Not without flying on a plane or driving several days."

"A plane?" That perked the boy's interest. "I've never been on a plane."

Most of Kaleb's experiences had included being flown in and out of various countries on military cargo planes or choppers. He offered a smile and thought it was time to change the subject since flying in a plane probably wasn't in the kid's immediate future. "It can be fun to fly, sure. But why did you come out here, Tommy?" He inched closer. "To get away from everyone?"

"Yeah. I didn't want to watch that stupid girl movie." Tommy turned away to look at the backyard. This section of the roof didn't overlook the pool; the master suite held that view. Instead, this area overlooked the backyard.

From this vantage point, Kaleb could see his net in the trio of palm trees. A trap yet to be sprung on the dark-haired guy.

"Go away," Tommy said abruptly. Kaleb held his breath

as the kid moved farther down the roof, putting more distance between them. "I wanna be alone."

"Tommy, you and I are the two men in the house." Kaleb eased closer. "It's up to us to protect the women and the girls, right? I need your help to keep them safe."

The boy glanced over his shoulder. "Me?"

It broke Kaleb's heart to realize how desperately Tommy needed a father figure. One that didn't lash out, giving him a black eye. "Yeah. Come on, give me a hand. Us guys need to stick together. I'm a little outnumbered here, don't you think?"

Tommy nodded slowly. "Yeah. I guess I can do that."

Kaleb breathed a small sigh of relief as he moved closer to Tommy. When Tommy turned to crawl up toward him, his foot slipped, and he fell to his stomach. Kaleb lunged forward, grabbing the boy's arm.

"I've got you." He slowly drew the boy toward him. Over Tommy's head, he saw movement along the edge of the property. Kaleb froze, narrowing his gaze until he could make out the figure of a man standing near the corner of the neighboring house.

The guy lifted his arm. When Kaleb saw the gun, he reacted within seconds. Pulling his Sig Sauer, he fired at the man, the gun reverberating loudly, while leaning forward to cover Tommy's body with his. The figure spun away and disappeared.

"What's going on?" Charlotte cried.

Kaleb didn't answer, his gaze riveted on the spot where he'd seen the dark-haired guy. He quickly scooped Tommy off the roof and lunged toward the window. "Crawl inside," he told the boy.

Tommy scrambled through the opening. Kaleb turned and took another moment to sweep his gaze over the backyard, but he didn't see any sign of the dark-haired guy. He heard Charlotte calling the police as Willow clutched Tommy in her arms.

He shimmied through the window, then raced out of the bedroom and down the stairs. Keying the alarm code in to leave took precious seconds. He stepped outside, shouting, "Set the alarm," before he ran in a crouch around to the back of the property.

Kaleb avoided his trip wires, and he rushed to the spot where he'd seen the gunman. A small reddish-brown stain on the side of the neighbor's house caught his attention.

Blood.

He'd wounded the perp. Not enough to slow him down, apparently. Kaleb inspected the ground for a blood trail and smiled with grim satisfaction when he found it. The drops of blood led through the neighbor's backyard, to the next one, then to the street located behind that.

The same path he'd taken the previous night when he'd spotted the mud-spattered plates on the black truck.

He scowled when the trail led to a spot at the side of the road. The puddle was larger there, and in his mind's eye, Kaleb imagined the guy dripping blood as he struggled to get inside the truck. Or whatever vehicle he was currently driving.

Unwilling to miss a possible trick, Kaleb ran down the street in the same direction the truck had taken the previous night. He didn't find any more blood, or anything else to indicate the guy had pulled over at some point.

He pushed forward, checking the next few streets, before giving up the chase. Wounding the guy must have scared him off. Kaleb only wished he'd done enough damage to prevent the guy from getting away. Not to kill him but to incapacitate him long enough to get him into custody.

Reluctantly, Kaleb turned around. No doubt the guy was long gone. The wail of sirens indicated the police would be at the safe house very soon. He jogged back, ignoring the ache in his knee.

The police needed to know to check out all the local hospitals. Gunshot wounds were required to be reported to the police, but he wasn't entirely sure if the guy's wound would be easily identified as such.

If he'd only grazed the guy, the doc on duty may not bother to report it. How many hospitals were in the area? He had no clue.

The squad was pulling into the driveway when he arrived. Charlotte was outside too.

He'd holstered his weapon but made sure to keep his hands in view as he approached and identified himself. "My name is Kaleb Tyson, I'm a retired Navy SEAL, and I've spoken several times to Detective Wales. He's aware of a man stalking the women and children staying here."

"He's armed!" one of the cops shouted.

Kaleb lifted his hands higher. "Yes, sir. I have a permit to carry a gun. It's a Sig Sauer, and I have a knife too."

One of the cops scuttled forward to take his gun. Kaleb wasn't surprised, but he'd hoped Wales would have responded so they could forgo all this. He wasn't the threat here, the guy he'd shot, the same guy who'd almost taken a shot at him and Tommy, was the one to be concerned about.

"Kaleb, are you okay?" Charlotte's concern warmed his heart.

He nodded, waiting patiently as the cop found and removed his knife too. He focused on the officer. "The gunman got away, but I wounded him. You need to put all the area hospitals on alert."

"This gun is warm and smells of gunpowder," the cop said. "You're the gunman."

"He is not," Charlotte said firmly. "Kaleb has been protecting us for several days from a man who shot twice at our previous safe house and then followed us here."

Kaleb reined in his frustration. "Please call Detective Wales. He'll fill you in on the case."

The sound of a vehicle coming down the road drew his attention. Kaleb spun toward it, staring at the ugly brown sedan. An unmarked car if he ever saw one, but he had never met Detective Wales face-to-face, so he didn't recognize the man behind the wheel. When he slid out of the car, Kaleb saw the gold badge clipped to his belt.

"Stand down, I've got this." The cop who appeared to be his age, maybe a year or two younger, walked toward him. "Kaleb Tyson?"

"Yes, sir." He was glad to lower his arms. "The gunman was here, lifted his weapon to fire at me, endangering a young boy, so I fired at him first, hoping to distract him. I wounded him and followed the blood trail to the road. You need to call the local hospitals to give them a heads-up."

"I see." Wales turned to the local cops. "Give him his gun back. Let's check out the scene."

"Hold on," the cop who took his gun and knife protested. "How do we know a kid's life was in danger? Maybe the former SEAL got trigger happy for no good reason."

"I saw the whole thing," Charlotte quickly interjected. "I'm happy to provide my statement, but please do as Kaleb asked. Notify the hospitals. This man has tried several times to harm us."

"Do it," Wales said to the cop. Then he turned back to Kaleb. "Show me the blood trail, but then start over at the beginning."

Kaleb nodded, shooting a reassuring smile at Charlotte. As he led the way around to the back of the house, staying clear of his trip wires, Kaleb silently prayed the gunman would be found at one of the local hospitals.

Tommy, Willow, and the others deserved to feel safe.

---

CHARLOTTE HAD to go through the sequence of events twice because the officer kept interrupting her. When he finally understood Tommy's role in all of this, he seemed satisfied, especially after she brought Willow out to talk to him as well.

Detective Wales had requested a crime scene tech respond to get samples of the blood left behind. She moved closer to Kaleb. "Do you think the blood will be enough to convince Grimes to get the DNA from the hat too? If he can match the blood to the DNA on the hat, that should give us this guy's identity."

"You read my mind." Kaleb displayed his phone. Grimes name was on the screen. "Calling him now."

"Good." She blew out a breath. This could be the break they needed. She wasn't sure if it was a good thing Tommy had climbed out onto the roof or not. If he hadn't, Kaleb may not have wounded the guy.

But on the other hand, if Tommy hadn't done something so dangerous, it was likely the dark-haired guy may have come close enough to become entangled in Kaleb's trap.

*Trust the Lord with all your heart and lean not on your*

*own understanding.*

The phrase reverberated through her mind. Charlotte straightened, remembering how Kaleb had encouraged her not to question God's plan.

Not an easy task to put herself in the Lord's hands. Yet she also knew God had sent Kaleb to help her. To watch over them.

To rescue Tommy from the roof.

To be in the right place at the right time to wound the gunman.

"Charlotte?" Milly joined her outside. "What time should I make dinner?"

Food was the last thing on her mind, but the others would be hungry, especially the kids. "Now is fine, Milly. I think the police are wrapping things up."

"Okay." Milly glanced at the police with uncertainty before turning to go back inside.

Fifteen minutes later, the two responding officers and the crime scene techs left. Kaleb had been given his gun and knife back without further problems. Wales was on the phone, and when he finished, he came toward them.

"That was Detective Grimes. He's putting your request for a DNA match on both the hat and the blood in front of the judge first thing in the morning."

"Thanks." Kaleb pulled the bag with the hat out of his pocket. "Any chance we can keep a section of the hat for Sierra? She's been doing a great job following the scent trail."

"Oh yeah." Wales glanced at Sierra. The dog had been barking like mad inside, so Kaleb had gone to get her. "I forgot about that."

"Please," Charlotte added. "We may need that if this guy comes back."

"I doubt he'll do that, especially now that he's injured," Wales protested. "Only a fool would return to the scene of the crime."

"This man hasn't been stopped coming after us yet," she retorted. "Are you really willing to risk putting the women and children staying here in harm's way?"

Wales let out a heavy sigh. "Okay, fine. But tampering with evidence could provide trouble for us later."

"Thank you," Kaleb said quietly. "I know this is an unusual request."

"Ya think?" Wales muttered. With a resigned expression, he drew on a pair of gloves and held a second pair out to Kaleb. Between them, they used Kaleb's knife to saw a jagged section of the hat away.

"This should work fine," Kaleb said, stuffing the baggie back into his pocket.

"I'll ask the patrol sergeant to make sure there are routine patrols through this area," Wales said. "Try not to shoot at any of them."

Kaleb's features tightened. "I would never discharge my weapon unless absolutely necessary, and never aiming toward a member of law enforcement."

Wales waved a hand. "Sorry, bad humor. I trust you, Tyson. If I didn't, I would have hauled you in by now."

"Thank you for allowing Kaleb to continue protecting us," Charlotte said. "We feel much safer having him here acting as a bodyguard." She glanced down at the dog hovering near Kaleb's side. "Sierra too."

The detective's expression softened just a bit. "You're welcome."

Charlotte turned to Kaleb. "We should go inside, Milly is probably holding dinner for us."

He nodded. Then he caught her by surprise, drawing

her into his arms for a quick hug. "You were great, Charlotte. Not only did you keep Willow calm while I spoke with Tommy, but you called the police."

She clung to him for a long moment, wishing she never had to let him go. But, of course, they couldn't stay out here. "You were the one who was amazing, Kaleb. Tommy really opened up to you."

"I feel for the kid," he admitted. He keyed in the code and opened the door. The moment they were safe inside, he activated the alarm. "This hasn't been easy for him."

"I know." The situation wasn't easy for any of the women here, but it was definitely worse for Willow and Tommy. Frustrating that Grimes hadn't found Thomas Acker yet. "No other news from Los Angeles?"

"No sign of Acker or Rodney Jones." Kaleb shook his head. "I know Los Angeles is a big city, but it shouldn't be this hard to find two suspects."

She felt the same way, but there was nothing more she could do about it now. As they walked into the kitchen, Kaleb sniffed the air appreciatively.

"Is that roasted chicken?" he asked with a grin.

Milly beamed. "Yes. Sit down, please, before the food gets cold."

The women and children were already at the table, including Tommy and Willow. Tommy grinned at Kaleb, and the two of them slapped high fives as Kaleb went by.

"I—uh, would like to say grace," Willow said when they were all seated.

"Sounds good," Kaleb encouraged.

Willow bowed her head and held Tommy's hand in hers. "Lord, we thank You for this fine meal we are about to eat. And also for sending Kaleb to protect us and to rescue Tommy when he needed it the most."

"Amen," Kaleb said.

"Amen," Charlotte echoed.

"Aw, Mom," Tommy muttered, "I was fine."

The mood around the table lightened as dishes were passed and plates were filled with Milly's latest creation. Simple fare, really, but better than many of these women have tasted in a long time.

It was difficult to keep her gaze off Kaleb. The man was truly remarkable, rescuing Tommy, then protecting the boy with his own body while firing at the assailant. Then he'd grabbed the boy, tucking him through the window.

The entire scene could have been taken straight from an action-adventure movie. Only the bullets and the danger had been terrifyingly real.

"After dinner, Tommy and I would like to watch the movie *Cars*," Kaleb announced.

The little boy beamed. "Really? *Cars*?"

"Yep." Kaleb glanced at Willow who was watching him in awe. "If that's okay with your mom."

"I—yes, it's fine," Willow managed.

It occurred to Charlotte that Willow deserved a man like Kaleb. A decent, kind, caring man who would care for Tommy as if the boy were his.

Kaleb caught Charlotte's gaze and smiled, and for a moment, she imagined what it would be like to have a man like Kaleb in her life.

No, not any man. Kaleb. Only Kaleb.

Of course, that wasn't meant to be. She knew it and so did he. But it didn't keep her from longing for something well out of her reach.

A family of her own.

Impossible. For one thing, her biological clock was too

far gone. Besides, having a family would mean giving up her mission of keeping women and children safe.

No. She couldn't do that. Not after a similar safe house had saved her life. Deep down, Charlotte knew that if Jerry had found her, she'd be dead.

Enough. There was no reason to want something out of reach. Not when she had these women and children to care for.

It was Kim's turn to do dishes, so the rest of the group returned to the recreational room to watch the movie *Cars*. Tommy led the way, looking like the king of the mountain with Kaleb at his side.

Abby, her donor, called. Charlotte hurried back upstairs so she could talk to the former congressman's wife in private. "Hi, Abby."

"Charlotte, you'll be glad to hear I've secured additional funding. Enough to turn a warehouse on the other side of town into a safe house, much like the one you've been living in. All windows will be located high on the walls, letting in light without allowing anyone to access them."

"Wow, that's amazing." Charlotte gazed around their plush surroundings. This wasn't reality, their previous safe house, and this new one Abby described, was where they belonged. "How long before we can use it?"

"I'm putting a rush on the renovations," Abby said. "But the earliest possible time frame to move in is two weeks."

"Maybe we should hold off on that idea," Charlotte said. "The police should have this guy arrested by then, and we can just go back to our old location."

"Are you sure?" Abby asked.

She felt someone behind her and turned to find Kaleb standing there. He held up his phone, showing her that Grimes was calling. She nodded in understanding. "Abby, I have to take another call, I'll get back to you soon, okay?" Without waiting for Abby to answer, she disconnected from the line.

"Tyson," Kaleb said, answering Grimes's call. "I'm putting you on speaker so Charlotte can hear."

"Detective Grimes? Do you have an update for us?" She held Kaleb's gaze as she spoke.

"Yes. We have Thomas Acker in custody," Grimes said.

"Thank You, Lord," Charlotte whispered.

"Has he sustained a gunshot wound or been grazed by a bullet?" Kaleb asked. "He left a trail of blood behind, so it has to be enough to need some level of medical attention."

"Unfortunately, he doesn't have any wounds, and we made him strip down to his skivvies after we brought him in," Grimes said dryly. "I'm getting a warrant to test his blood to see if it's the same type as found at your safe house, but getting even a basic blood type match will take time."

Charlotte closed her eyes, her hopes deflating like a punctured balloon. "Does that mean you don't think he's our gunman?"

"I'm not sure he is," Grimes admitted. "He didn't have a gun on him when we picked him up, he's not wounded, and we didn't find a weapon in his apartment either. Acker claims he has an alibi for the time frame of the shooting earlier today, so we'll check that out." There was a pause before Grimes added, "My gut is telling me this isn't our guy."

No gun, no injury, and a possible alibi. She stared at Kaleb. "If the gunman isn't Thomas Acker, then who is he?"

Kaleb shook his head. "I don't know."

Her knees threatened to buckle beneath a wave of despair. They were back at square one, with no clue who the gunman was or which of them he'd targeted.

# CHAPTER THIRTEEN

"Any chance we can get Acker's DNA?" Kaleb asked Grimes.

"Don't have enough evidence for a warrant," Grimes pointed out. "I can ask, see if he'll cooperate."

"Maybe he will, just to clear his name." A vain hope, really, as Kaleb knew anyone who would abuse a woman and child wasn't likely to cooperate with law enforcement.

"Don't hold your breath," Grimes muttered. "Let me know if your perp shows up in Agoura Hills."

"Yeah, I will." After he contacted the locals, Kaleb added silently, "Thanks, Detective."

Charlotte whirled away and stumbled toward the sofa. She collapsed onto it, burying her face in her hands.

"Hey, don't be upset." Kaleb sat and wrapped his arms around her. "Think of it this way, we can assure Willow and Tommy that they're safe."

"Are they?" Charlotte lifted her head, her aquamarine eyes swimming with tears. "If the dark-haired guy returns, I don't think he'll care how many of the women and children get hurt."

"Yes, that is a possibility," he agreed. "But you must know I'm not going to let that happen."

"For how long?" Charlotte shook her head. "You've put your life on hold for days, Kaleb. Now that this guy is injured, he could lay low. Hide out for a while. Maybe regroup and come back after us in a few days or a few weeks." She pulled out of his arms and jumped to her feet. "I need to call my donor. She'll help us get relocated. That may be our only way to stay safe."

"Hold on." Kaleb reached out and tugged her back down. "Let's talk this through. We still have five days here. The security alarm has been working pretty well, especially with my additional security measures. Give me a few more days before you set up a new place. I'm sure that money could be saved for a problem down the road."

She swiped at her eyes and sighed. "It feels like the police are never going to find this guy."

Privately, Kaleb agreed. He'd had more interaction with this guy than any of the officers had. Yet he'd failed in his mission to grab him. Kaleb wished he'd followed his gut and had called Senior Chief, Nico, or any of the others to help. He'd really hoped Hudson would respond to his call for help, especially since he'd asked for backup rather than just checking in on the guy.

But so far there had been no response. Either Hudson was so far off-grid his phone wasn't working. Or the guy wasn't in a position to call him back.

He prayed Hudson, who'd suffered a devastating injury after the underwater bomb had exploded, would be okay. Not just physically, as the blindness in his left eye was permanent, but emotionally.

Spiritually.

"I'll wait until tomorrow to decide next steps," Charlotte said, drawing him from his thoughts. "It's not like they'll start renovations at this hour."

"What kind of renovations?"

"She found a warehouse, much like the previous safe house, that is available for rent, but the interior needs work." She shrugged. "At a minimum, we need a small kitchen and a few bedrooms, with numerous beds for our residents."

He nodded, humbled by the fact that they were asking for so little. It shouldn't be this difficult to keep them safe. Yet he knew more than most how terribly evil people could be. He stroked Sierra's fur. "Thanks for putting your faith in me, Charlotte."

She managed a smile. "If you would have asked me four days ago to trust a man with the lives of these women and children, I'd have flat-out refused. But you proved to be the exception to the rule, Kaleb."

"I'm not, there are plenty of decent men in the world." At least, that's what he wanted to believe. "You and I have had the misfortune of seeing the worst in people. We shouldn't let our personal experiences cloud our judgment of the general population."

"You're right." She drew in a deep breath. "Thanks for the reminder."

He drew her in for a quick hug, then forced himself to move away. Charlotte was a distraction he couldn't afford. Not now. There was a distinct possibility that he'd angered the gunman enough to make him return to exact his revenge. And deep in his gut, Kaleb hoped he would.

This time, he'd be ready.

"I need to take Sierra outside." He called the dog over. "We'll walk the perimeter again, so it may take a while."

"Okay. In the meantime, I'll let Willow know that her husband isn't the one coming after us."

He hoped Willow would find some comfort in that. Although he doubted the woman would relax until they had the dark-haired guy in custody and they were back in their original safe house.

After disarming the alarm, he took Sierra outside. After reactivating the alarm, he stood near the front door, listening intently.

This neighborhood was unusually quiet. There was no sign of the occupants of the house to the right, the one the dark-haired guy used to access their backyard.

Were all of these houses used primarily as vacation rentals? It would explain why very little traffic came down this street. Other than the two women who'd argued about their plans, he hadn't seen anyone milling about. Yet it seemed like a waste of expensive real estate.

Sierra waited patiently for him to move away from the doorway. He went to the pool side of the property first, sweeping his gaze over the area. There wasn't enough foliage for him to set up additional trip wires there. He lifted his gaze, noting the windows of the master suite were dark. Then he turned to check the sight line from the master suite to the adjacent property.

That home looked dark, too, but there were two large windows facing the master suite.

He continued moving along the perimeter, identifying a couple of spots he could add trip wires. Keeping Sierra close so she didn't trigger any of them, he continued making his way around the house.

The net was still suspended up in the leaves of the trio of palm trees. If the dark-haired guy returned, he hoped the net would hold him long enough for Kaleb to grab him.

If the guy managed to trigger the net trap at all.

The evening was quiet, the sun setting low on the horizon. Kaleb went back inside the house, grabbed more fishing line, then returned to set up the additional wires.

His phone rang as he was finishing up. He nearly dropped it when he recognized Hudson's name on the screen. "Hudd? Hey, man, are you okay?"

"You need help?" The curt tone did not invite further questions related to his health status.

"I could use some backup," Kaleb agreed, still shocked his teammate had called. "I'm protecting a group of abused women and children from a gunman who has tried several times to break in."

"Where?"

"We're in a suburb of Los Angeles called Agoura Hills. Where are you?"

"Boise."

Kaleb frowned, wondering why on earth Hudd was in Idaho. The guy had lived in the San Diego area for years, as they all had while in the navy. Easier that way, especially when they were called up at a moment's notice. "That's pretty far away."

"Thirteen to fourteen hours by car, possibly more depending on traffic." Hudd's voice was terse. "I'll aim to be there in the morning."

"Ah, okay, if you're sure." He didn't want to refuse Hudd's help, especially since the guy had been off-grid for so long. "I would appreciate having backup. We're staying in a rental property with a security system, and I've added additional traps to prevent anyone from getting too close. Call me when you're thirty minutes out."

"Okay." The call ended as abruptly as it had begun.

Kaleb stared at his phone, then dialed Mason's number. "Chief? I heard from Hudd, he's on his way to help me out."

"Where has he been?" Mason Gray demanded.

"Boise, Idaho. Don't ask me why, Hudd wasn't exactly chatty."

"Is he going to be able to get to you in time?" Mason asked. "If you needed backup, you should have called me."

"I was going to, but I've had things under control." Mostly under control. "If you want to know the truth, I called Hudd hoping a request for backup would be enough to draw him out of hiding."

"Hmm. I guess that part worked." Mason paused, then added, "I can help too."

It was tempting, but even if Mason left now, it would be four to five hours before he'd get there. "Nah, I'll be fine tonight. I managed to wound the perp earlier today. I'm hoping he'll get picked up at a local hospital sooner than later."

"Sounds like things have been dicey," Mason drawled.

"I haven't been bored, that's for sure," he replied wryly. "How are you?"

"Living the dream," Mason said without hesitation. "And I mean that with all my heart. I couldn't be happier with my beautiful wife, Aubrey, and our son, Lucas."

Another reason Kaleb hadn't asked their former team leader for help. And for the first time, he felt a twinge of envy. Not that he begrudged Senior Chief anything, but thinking about Charlotte made him realize he wanted something similar.

But that was impossible. Not just because he'd promised to help Nico find Ava but because Charlotte didn't want that kind of relationship with him.

"I'm happy for you, Chief."

"Thanks, Kaleb. Maybe I should head up tomorrow? I'd like to check in on Hudson."

He wouldn't have minded more hands, but he wasn't

sure how the women and children inside might feel about that. "Hang tight for now, Chief. If we need more hands, I'll let you know. I'd rather not scare the women and children seeking refuge from physical abuse by bringing in a whole team of men."

"Roger that. But next time, don't hesitate to call," Mason chided.

"I won't, Chief. Thanks." He ended the call, feeling optimistic. Hudd was alive and willing to help. Mason had settled down into his new life.

He lifted his gaze to the sky. Several stars were visible now that the sun had faded away.

"Dear Lord, please keep Hudson and our other teammates safely in Your care. Amen."

After making one more sweep of the perimeter, he headed inside. He wanted to make sure everyone was settled in for the night before he returned to find a place to sit and wait for their perp to show up.

With God's grace, he'd prefer to have the gunman caught and turned over to the police before Hudson arrived. If so, he'd strong-arm Hudd into traveling with him to San Diego to meet up with Mason. Maybe even convince Hudd to help him pick up Ava Rampart's trail.

Whether Hudd like it or not. Because reconnecting with friends, with guys that were closer than most brothers, was the best way to get through troubling times.

Something he'd need too. Leaving Charlotte wouldn't be easy. There wasn't a doubt in Kaleb's mind that he'd leave a large part of his heart behind once he was forced to move on.

WILLOW HAD BEEN RELIEVED to hear Thomas Acker wasn't the guy who'd been outside their safe house. Charlotte had reminded her, though, that they still needed to be on guard until the gunman had been caught. Willow solemnly agreed.

The house felt empty without Kaleb. Her fault for growing dependent on him. For allowing herself to become accustomed to having him around.

She'd promised to wait until tomorrow to call Abby, but she knew moving to another location was the right thing to do. Yes, the money Abby had raised would have gone to better use in providing clothing and other relocation services to her residents, but those were secondary issues.

The primary goal was to keep them alive.

Over the next hour, many of the women retired to their rooms. Tommy had practically fallen asleep next to Willow, so she'd urged them to go upstairs too. Milly joined her in the kitchen, stifling a yawn.

"I'm ready for bed," she announced.

Charlotte forced a smile. "Go ahead, get some rest. I'm going to make some tea before I head up."

Milly frowned. "I've noticed you haven't been sleeping much."

*True that*, she thought ruefully. "It's been stressful with this guy constantly coming after us."

"Charlotte, you should learn to give your worries over to God." Milly patted her arm. "And Kaleb is here to protect us."

"I know." She knew Kaleb would do whatever was necessary to keep them safe. "It's just—I have a lot on my mind."

"Hand your troubles over to God," Milly repeated. "He will carry those burdens for you."

She tipped her head, regarding the older woman thoughtfully. "You've never mentioned God and prayer before."

Milly flushed. "I should have. I was raised to believe in God but somehow let go of my faith. Then Kaleb arrived, bringing his faith and prayers to our table. That handsome young man made me realize I shouldn't have strayed."

Charlotte knew Milly had suffered abuse too. Maybe not as detrimental as some of them, her husband had been an alcoholic, ragging at her when he was drunk. His swings at her had rarely connected, but Milly had admitted to staying with him longer than she should have.

"Didn't James attend church too?" Charlotte asked.

Milly waved a hand. "Going to church doesn't mean anything. God isn't in church, He is here, in our hearts." She rested her palm on her chest. "Trust me, James didn't have God in his heart."

Charlotte nodded, knowing Jerry hadn't had God in his heart either. Not that Jerry had ever crossed the threshold of a church. "I guess you're right."

"Now Kaleb? That man has God in his heart." Milly wagged a finger. "I've seen the way you look at him, Char. Don't let that man go without a fight."

"Milly, he's not my man to fight over," she protested.

"He could be," Milly insisted. "I've noticed the way he looks at you too."

She felt her cheeks flush and quickly moved to the cabinet for her Sleepytime tea. "Enough, Milly. Get some sleep. I'll be up shortly."

Milly's gaze bored into her back for a long moment before the woman moved away. Charlotte heated up a mug of water in the microwave, grateful for something to do.

Kaleb hadn't come back inside. Sierra was stretched out near the front door, patiently waiting for him to return. Charlotte dunked her Sleepytime tea bag into the hot water, wondering if she was using the tea as an excuse to do the same.

The day had been mentally exhausting. Yet thoughts continued to whirl in her mind. Between her growing feelings for Kaleb, worry over the gunman, and Abby's offer to renovate another warehouse to use as their future safe house, she highly doubted she'd be able to sleep.

Sierra abruptly lifted her head and scrambled to her feet. Charlotte frowned, then relaxed when she saw the alarm had been deactivated. Seconds later, Kaleb appeared, quickly keying in the code.

"Good girl," he said, greeting Sierra who was wiggling with excitement as if Kaleb had been gone for months rather than ninety minutes.

"Everything quiet outside?"

His gaze caught hers. "Yeah, so far. But I'm thinking of staying outside most of the night in case this guy shows up again."

She frowned. "But I thought that was why you set up the trip wires? So that you didn't have to stay outside."

"I want to get this guy, Charlotte." He shrugged, his expression grim. "The best way to do that is to be ready and waiting for him."

As much as she hated the idea of him being out in the cold, she knew he was right. Except for the fact that this guy was injured, which made it less likely he'd return so quickly. "You really think he'll show up?"

"It's always better to be prepared."

She sipped her tea. "I can give you a pillow and blanket."

He grinned. "Thanks, but that won't work. I need to stay hidden from view."

"Oh, sure. Of course." She felt like an idiot.

"I wouldn't mind coffee, though," he said. In a flash, she was transported back to the first night they'd met. When he'd calmly agreed to stay outside all night to keep them safe. Asking for nothing more than a cup of coffee in return.

Going with her instincts, she'd trusted him. A gesture that had provided the best possible outcome. He'd saved them more than once.

She moved away from the kitchen counter so fast she spilled her tea. "I'll get a pot brewing right away."

"No rush." Kaleb came to join her. "I'm sure he'll wait until much later, when he thinks we're at our most vulnerable."

She raised a brow, filling the carafe with water. "No one who knows you would think you're vulnerable."

"Maybe not after the way I wounded him, but some people's actions defy logic," Kaleb responded.

"True." Certainly, the way this guy kept coming after them defied logic. Why he couldn't just give up and move on was a mystery. Didn't the gunman realize his own life was on the line? What was the point of revenge if doing so landed you in jail?

Then again, most abusers acted as if they were above the law. And some of them, like Abby's congressman husband, had been untouchable.

Jerry, too, had his cop brother on his side. He believed the picture Jerry had painted of Charlotte as a crazy woman who had attacked him, forcing him to defend himself.

Yeah, right.

She shook off the depressing thoughts, focusing her gaze on the coffee maker. "This should be ready in ten minutes."

Kaleb nodded, watching her intently for a long moment before turning away. "I'll be back soon."

Charlotte sipped her lukewarm tea, listening to the drip, drip, drip of the coffee. If Kaleb was going to spend the night outside, maybe she'd sleep on the sofa. That way, she wouldn't have to listen to Milly's snoring.

And she'd be close at hand if Kaleb needed her.

The last thought made her grimace. Kaleb wouldn't need her other than maybe to call 911, the way she had when Tommy had been out on the roof.

Still, her meager presence had to be better than no one backing him up.

She decided to head back upstairs to grab her .38. Tiptoeing into the room, she silently opened the drawer next to her side of the bed and withdrew the gun. Milly mumbled something in her sleep as Charlotte removed the trigger lock.

She grabbed her pillow from the bed and carried both items back downstairs. In the living room, she tossed her pillow onto one end of the sofa, bringing her gun into the kitchen with her.

Having the weapon was a necessity, but that didn't mean she'd gotten comfortable in carrying it around. Thankfully, her sweater had deep pockets.

"You look ready to take on anyone who dares to enter," Kaleb drawled as he joined her.

She tried not to show her discomfort in having the weapon weighing her down. "I'll sleep on the sofa tonight, in case you need me."

He frowned. "No reason to do that."

"There's every reason," she countered. The coffeepot finished brewing, so she rummaged in the cupboards until she found the same insulated mug she'd used that first night.

Milly must have brought it with them in the box of kitchen goods. "I plan to call the police if I hear anything unusual."

He hesitated, then nodded. "Okay, but I still think you should sleep in a regular bed."

"Says the man who has spent two nights on a short sofa and is now planning to stay outside all night," she retorted. After filling the mug, she handed it to him. "Are you taking Sierra with you?"

"Not this time." A tingle of awareness shot up her arm when their fingers brushed. He took the mug and smiled gratefully. "The trip wires may prove a problem for her. Besides, I'd rather she stay inside to guard you."

She didn't like that idea, but there was no point in arguing. She suspected the real reason Kaleb wanted his dog to stay inside was to keep Sierra out of the line of fire.

He turned to head for the door.

"Kaleb? Wait." She hurried around the edge of the counter. Resting her hand on his arm, she went up on her toes and pressed a kiss to his cheek. "Please be careful."

"This is nothing for you to worry about." His voice was low and husky, his dark eyes reassuring. "I've been in far more dangerous situations than this."

"I know. I just—want you to be safe." She caught herself before she could blurt out the truth.

That she was falling in love with him.

"You too, Charlotte." He surprised her by pressing a heated kiss on her upturned mouth. The embrace was over before it started. And when he released her, she had to fight off the urge to cling to him.

He deactivated the alarm and stepped outside. She quickly crossed the room to activate it again.

Sierra gazed up at her with a questioning look.

"It's just you and me, girl," she whispered, smoothing a

hand over the dog's silky fur. "We have to trust that God will watch over him."

Sierra licked her wrist as if in agreement.

Charlotte downed the last of her cold tea, washed the mug, and returned it to the cupboard. Sierra followed like a dark shadow as she moved from the kitchen to the living room. And when Charlotte stretched out on the sofa, Sierra assumed a similar position on the floor right in front of her.

She tucked the .38 beneath her pillow and tried to sleep. After several moments, she turned to prayer.

*Lord, I know I'm not worthy to ask anything of You, but please keep Kaleb safe in Your care this night. Amen.*

Somehow, she must have drifted off because a strange noise brought her bolt upright. She pulled the gun from beneath the pillow, aiming the barrel at the front door.

*Was someone out there?*

## CHAPTER FOURTEEN

Tucked up against the corner of the building, Kaleb heard the distant sound of a car engine minutes before he saw the reflection of twin headlights in the neighbor's window. When the rumble of the vehicle grew louder, he set his mug of coffee aside and silently crept along the edge of the property.

A sedan pulled into the driveway. He didn't move for long seconds until the driver of the vehicle slid out from behind the wheel. Seeing the familiar features of Detective Wales made him relax.

The detective slammed the car door shut. Then the guy startled badly, grabbing for his gun when Kaleb stepped out from around the corner of the house.

"You shouldn't sneak up on a cop like that, Tyson," Wales chided, lowering his hand from his weapon. "That's a good way to get shot."

"Sorry," Kaleb said, although truthfully, he hadn't done anything wrong. If the detective would shoot at a moving shadow without knowing who the person was, especially in a residential area, he needed to go back to the police academy. But Kaleb didn't voice his thoughts. "Obviously, I'm trying to keep an eye on things in case our perp returns to finish the job. What brings you here?"

"We found the stolen truck," Wales informed him. "The crime scene techs are in the process of gathering evidence. Looks like it was wiped down, but the tech has lifted a couple of decent prints from the handle of the driver's seat adjuster and the inside of the driver's side door handle. Those are key spots where your average criminal doesn't think to wipe down. We also contacted the truck's rightful owner. He's agreed to be fingerprinted so we can rule him out."

Fingerprints were more than Kaleb could have hoped for, and he was glad to hear they'd checked those locations. "That's great news. Where did you find it?"

Wales grimaced. "I hate to admit this, but the truck was found just a few blocks away from this safe house. It was parked in a driveway, so no one looked at it twice. Until the homeowners returned and called it in."

Kaleb scowled. "Could be that he chose that location after doing some recon. It's the only way he could know the homeowners were gone."

"Maybe." Wales shrugged. "There are a lot of rentals around here, so he may have just dumped it in plain sight, hoping for the best."

"Why are there so many rentals?" Kaleb asked. "It's weird."

Wales shook his head. "Not sure, although when the Airbnb phase took off, these homes were in high demand. I guess many of these places are second homes for the rich and famous. I'm sure the extra income gained from renting them out helps pay the property taxes and other annual expenses."

That was a world Kaleb couldn't imagine living in. He turned to more important matters. "How soon can you get the prints from the truck run through the system?"

"The truck owner is coming in first thing in the morning. Hopefully, we'll have something shortly thereafter."

"You could run the prints tonight, without waiting for the owner to come in. I doubt the guy has a criminal record." Kaleb knew he was being pushy, but this gunman has been on the loose long enough. Every hour of a delay was another hour the guy could try again.

A hit from the fingerprints they'd lifted from the stolen truck could break this case wide open.

"Kaleb? Is there a problem?" Charlotte asked.

He turned to see her hovering in the doorway. "Nothing to worry about, sorry if we woke you."

"I heard the car door slam." She stepped over the threshold. Wrapping her arms around her torso as if to ward off the chill in the air, she walked toward them. "Good evening, Detective Wales. Are you here because you've arrested the suspect?"

"Not yet," Wales admitted. "We found the truck he stole, though, and are in the process of checking for fingerprints."

"Really?" Charlotte's eyes flared with hope. "That's wonderful news. It would be so nice to feel safe."

Her words struck a chord with the detective. His expression softened, and he nodded. "I'll run them yet tonight, see if we get any hits. If we do, I'd like to show you some mug shots, see if you can identify him."

"Anytime," Charlotte agreed. "No matter how late. The sooner we figure out who this guy is, the better for all of us. The women and children living here have been on edge since the earlier shooting incident."

"That's why I'm staying outside," Kaleb reminded her. "To make sure you and the others are safe."

"I know." Charlotte offered a lopsided smile. "I feel bad you have to stay out here, though."

Her concern warmed his heart, even though it wasn't at all necessary. He'd spent way more time in far worse conditions. "I'm fine."

"Well, I'll head back then," Wales said. Then he looked directly at Kaleb. "Next time, I'll call before I swing by."

"Good idea," Kaleb agreed. "Better that way so Charlotte and the others won't be afraid."

"That was never my intent." Wales opened the driver's side door. "I'll let you know when I have news."

"No matter how late," Charlotte reminded with emphasis. "Please, it's not like I'm getting much sleep anyway."

"Understood." Wales slid behind the wheel, started the car, and backed out of the driveway.

"Do you think they'll find him from those fingerprints?" Charlotte asked, watching the taillights recede.

"I think it's a very good chance they will," Kaleb said reassuringly. He put his arm around her shoulders and guided her toward the door. "Go inside, you're shivering out here."

"I was scared spitless when I heard the thudding sound," she confided. "One minute I was asleep, the next I was holding my gun, aiming at the front door."

He winced. "I'm sorry you had to go through that, but your instincts were right on target. I'm glad you were ready and willing to do whatever was necessary."

"Yes." She sighed heavily. "It's just sad that it's come to this."

"Don't get discouraged." He pulled her in for a hug. "I feel like we're finally close to getting this guy."

She nodded, leaning against him for a long moment. As much as he would have loved nothing more than to cradle Charlotte in his arms, she was vulnerable out there. He gently nudged her to the door, entered the code, and opened it. "Get some sleep. And make sure to activate the alarm."

"Thanks, Kaleb." She disappeared inside.

Kaleb turned to scan the area. The hour wasn't that late, only nine o'clock at night. Still, he couldn't help but wonder if the detective had scared off the gunman. Getting a hit on his fingerprints in the system would be a huge first step. It would be additional evidence to put him at the scene once they had the guy behind bars.

It wasn't enough, though, for Kaleb to let his guard down. He couldn't shake the feeling this guy may be desperate enough to make another attempt tonight.

Sliding into the shadows was second nature. He moved along the house, every sense on alert. He would have liked to have had Sierra with him, but considering the trip wires, it was better for her to stay inside with Charlotte.

It bothered him to see his gun-toting pixie looking worn down and scared to death. Charlotte really needed a good night of sleep, but he sensed that was easier said than done. Especially now that she knew there was a potential lead.

He silently patrolled the perimeter of the property, finding nothing amiss. Then he retrieved his mug of coffee and settled at the corner of the house near the trio of palm trees, making himself as invisible as possible.

The next hour passed slowly. Sitting still for so long wasn't normally a problem, although he was reminded of his advanced age of forty at the constant ache in his right knee. A souvenir of that fateful night.

*No*, he silently warned. *Don't go there.* Delving into the past could trigger a flashback, and he couldn't afford the distraction.

Especially not tonight.

Ignoring the pain, he closed his eyes, listening intently to the sounds of the night. The wind rustling through the foliage was barely above a whisper. This neighborhood was unusually quiet, which was how he'd heard the detective's approach so easily.

Another thirty minutes passed. His knee was so painful he had to stand to ease the pressure. So much for being a stealthy Navy SEAL.

His phone vibrated in his pocket. Hudson's name flashed on the screen. "Hey, buddy, what's going on?"

"Hit traffic," Hudson said tersely. "We'll be late."

Hudd, a man of few words. "We? Oh, you mean Echo?" Hudson had gotten a golden brown German shepherd from the infamous dog rescuer, Lillian. It was the same place he'd gotten Sierra. Their master chief, Mason Gray, had found Lillian, a woman who specialized in providing highly intelligent and easily trained canines to veterans. The dogs often provided dual purposes, offering comfort and giving each of them a good way to adjust to civilian life after spending so much time in the military.

And when Lillian had learned about their last op, she'd insisted each team member take a dog. Kaleb knew Mason had slipped her money to support her cause, and he'd done the same, supporting her through her website after heading back to San Diego.

Sierra's love and devotion had helped keep him from becoming too immersed in his own problems. From wallowing in the depths of self-pity. He could only hope that Echo had done the same for Hudson.

"Yeah. Later." The phone went dead.

Kaleb smiled grimly and put the phone away. He was glad Hudson hadn't given up on joining him in favor of returning to Boise. And why Boise anyway? He made a mental note to ask Hudson about Idaho when he had the chance.

Another thirty minutes passed, and the area around the safe house remained quiet. Kaleb didn't lower his guard, even though he suspected the guy wouldn't make another move until well past midnight.

Their SEAL team had often struck their intended targets at zero three hundred hours. He had to figure nonmilitary perps would think along the same lines.

Nothing good happened after midnight.

His phone buzzed again, this time a text from Detective Wales. His heart sank as he read the message.

*No hit on prints in AFIS.*

He keyed in a response thanking him for the update. Charlotte would be disappointed that their one clue had fizzled out.

The way so many others had.

He moved toward the front of the property, narrowing his gaze when a brief flash of light caught his eye. He froze and stared for several long moments, waiting for it to return.

It didn't.

What had caused it? He'd checked the house direction across the street earlier that day, when he'd gone searching for the black truck. The place had been empty, no sign of anyone living there. Even now, the windows remained dark.

Had it been a reflection off a light up on the hillside? Maybe. He watched for another fifteen minutes before moving on. After completing his exterior patrol, he went up the steps to the front door. He punched in the key code and stepped inside. Charlotte was seated on the sofa, but she didn't have her gun in hand. Likely she'd assumed it was him because he'd entered the alarm code.

"Bad news," he told her after reengaging the alarm and greeting Sierra who was excited to see him. "Detective Wales didn't get any hits from the fingerprints in the truck. Whoever this guy is, he isn't in the system."

Her shoulders slumped. "I was hoping they'd have identified him by now."

"Me too." He tried to smile. "But there's still a chance he'll show up tonight. I came in to give you the news and to use the bathroom."

She nodded. "Of course."

Sierra tried to follow him inside, but he gave her the hand gesture for sit. "Guard," he commanded.

Sierra sat.

Five minutes later, he returned to the living room, Sierra at his side. The pillow on the couch made him frown. "I told you there's no need to sleep on the sofa."

"Why not? You did." She lifted her chin. "Besides, it's easier to back you up from down here."

He wanted to argue, but her logic was solid. If Hudson had been there, that's exactly where he would be. "Just remember your main job is to call 911, not to come outside armed with a gun, okay?"

She nodded but didn't say anything. He felt certain she'd do the first, but also come out to find him.

"Please, Charlotte. You're the last defense between the bad guy and the other women and children. You need to stay inside and keep them safe. I'm a SEAL, I can take care of myself."

"I know." She blew out a breath. "I'll protect them."

He decided there was no point in pushing the issue. If

he did his job right, she wouldn't have to do anything but make the 911 call. "Get some sleep, Charlotte."

"I'll try."

He gave Sierra one last pat, then went back outside. After entering the alarm, he headed back to the side of the house, the location where the perp had accessed the property at least three times previously.

It would be a long night.

---

"COME, SIERRA." Charlotte stretched out on the sofa, then slid her hand beneath the pillow, seeking the odd comfort of the weapon hiding there. If anyone had asked her ten years ago if she'd own a gun, she'd have laughed hysterically and vehemently denied such a thing.

Oh, how her life had changed.

Her childhood had been normal, her parents middle-class hard workers. She'd attended college, earning an accounting degree.

Rory, her first serious boyfriend, had broken her heart, and she'd avoided men and dating until she'd met Jerry. It burned now to realize how she'd fallen for the idea of love, hearth, and family rather than seeing the man clearly for who he was.

And who he wasn't.

Her parents were gone now, and she had no other family left. Except for the women and children who came through her shelter.

Thinking of the social workers who normally referred women to her made her realize she hadn't heard from them in the past few days. Normally she received at least one to two new residents a week. In reality, the number should be much higher, but all too often, women refused to seek shelter, preferring to go home with family or friends.

Only to ultimately end up back with their abuser.

Hadn't she done that same thing after the first time Jerry had hit her? It had been so inconceivable to her that he'd done that, she told herself it couldn't possibly happen again.

But it had. More than once.

A creaking noise on the steps behind her made her jolt. Twisting to look over her shoulder, she found Willow standing there.

"Why are you sleeping down here?" Willow asked with a frown.

"Milly snores." Charlotte figured it was better to downplay her own fears. "Looks like you're having trouble sleeping too."

"I keep thinking about Thomas," Willow confessed. "I know you said he has an alibi, but I still think he's going to come looking for me and Tommy."

"I understand," Charlotte said, thinking of her own situation. If Jerry hadn't found another woman to marry, she'd feel the same way. "Try not to worry, though. Remember, he's been warned off by the police."

Willow grimaced. "That hadn't necessarily stopped him before." She moved farther into the room. "I blame myself for what he did to Tommy. If I had acted sooner . . ." Her voice trailed off.

"Don't spend your life looking backward, Willow. Stay focused on the future. Tommy may have some adjustments to make, but he's doing well."

"I just wish I'd never gone back to Thomas after the first time he hurt me."

Charlotte could relate. "You're here now, Willow."

"Do you think he'll really give up trying to get me back?" Willow asked. "Thomas keeps claiming he's changed, but I'm afraid to believe him."

"Don't go back," Charlotte advised. "And you won't have to worry for much longer. As soon this current situation is resolved, we'll get you relocated to another safe house." She smiled reassuringly. "He won't find you or your son."

The slender woman nodded but didn't look entirely convinced. Then she glanced around. "Where's Kaleb?"

"Outside, keeping watch."

"All night?"

"Yes. But he assures me he's fine. No reason for us to worry."

Willow relaxed at this news. "He's a good man."

"Yes, he is." Charlotte squelched a surge of jealousy. Kaleb was a handsome single guy, she had no business feeling as if he belonged to her. If he wanted to date any of the women here, including Willow, he could. Especially once Willow and Tommy were relocated to a new place to live.

"You two would be great together," Willow said.

"What?" Her jaw dropped, and she had to force herself to close her mouth. "Oh, no. It's not like that. Kaleb is nice to all of us, not just me. Once the gunman has been caught, he'll move on. He's still searching for Ava, remember?"

"Maybe he'll stay with you." Willow lifted a brow. "Don't look so surprised. The possibility must have crossed your mind."

First Milly, now Willow. Charlotte hoped her feelings for Kaleb weren't as obvious to him as they apparently were to the women around her. "You know men aren't allowed in the safe house, so no, there is no possibility of that happening."

"But that's not like, a general safe house rule, is it?" Willow asked. "That's just your personal rule."

"Yes, because that's the right thing to do for those women seeking shelter. You remember how skittish you were being near the male police officers. Having a man around every day would be far worse." Why was she even having this discussion? There was no future for her and Kaleb, even if he wanted one. Which she was fairly sure he didn't.

She rose and faced Willow. "It's late. Why don't you head back upstairs? Tomorrow will likely be a busy day, especially if we have to move to another location." A strong possibility now that she knew the gunman wasn't likely to be identified anytime soon.

"Okay, but keep in mind, you shouldn't have to give up having a family of your own just to protect a bunch of strangers. Any of us could take your place in running the safe house, Charlotte." She paused, then added, "Even me. Good night." Willow turned and mounted the stairs to the second story.

Charlotte stared after her, perplexed by her words. Was Willow really concerned about her love life or lack thereof? Or was this the woman's way of saying how much she'd rather be managing the safe house? It hardly seemed likely to be the latter. For one thing, Charlotte couldn't imagine Willow learning how to use a gun.

No, more likely Willow was reluctant to move on with the next stage of her journey. One in which she'd be taken to a new location, receive help in finding a new job and a place for her and Tommy to live. It was a step that would force the young mother to move out of her comfort zone.

And back into society.

Charlotte moved through the house, going from one window to the next. Sierra padded along with her, no doubt taking her job as a protector seriously. Each time she peered into the darkness, she tried to find Kaleb. She never saw him. It was both reassuring and awe-inspiring.

The man was good, no question about that. She felt safe with him guarding them.

So why was she having so much trouble relaxing?

Giving herself a mental shake, she finally returned to the living room. Sierra stood looking up at her expectantly.

"I know, I'm a mess," she confided. "It's time we both get some sleep."

It wasn't until she stretched out on the sofa that Sierra lay down next to her. When the dog's eyes drifted closed as she fell asleep, Charlotte had to smile.

If only it was that easy for her to do the same.

She forced herself to close her eyes and relax. That first year after leaving the hospital, she'd wake up with night terrors. In every single one, she was helpless to escape as her ex-fiancé came after her.

Sierra let out a series of cute muffled barks. Charlotte lifted her head to look down at the dog, her front paws moving as she experienced happy doggy dreams.

There was a sound near the front door. Charlotte froze for a moment, then relaxed as the key code was entered. Kaleb must be coming back in to use the restroom. When the door opened, Sierra abruptly woke up, growling low in her throat.

Charlotte was surprised, Sierra had never growled when Kaleb came in. Then she froze as the door opened wider and a slender man with dark hair stepped inside, holding his gun pointed directly at her.

Sierra jumped to her feet, growling and barking at the gunman. Soon the rest of the house would be awake, and that wouldn't be good.

Charlotte subtly slid her right hand beneath the pillow to find the gun, even as she faced the man of her nightmares. She did her best to look nonchalant, even though her heart was hammering with fear. "Hello, Jerry."

"Shut that dog up or I'll shoot him," Jerry snapped. Not only had he dyed his hair, but his nose looked different, smaller somehow, and his cheekbones more pronounced. Looking at him now, she understood she should have suspected him all along. But she hadn't.

Charlotte reached out her left hand to the dog, hoping to calm the animal, while praying that Kaleb wasn't lying outside injured or worse—*dead*.

# CHAPTER FIFTEEN

Kaleb couldn't get that flash of light he'd noticed from the house across the street out of his mind. It took a full minute to understand why it bothered him.

It reminded him of the reflection off a rifle scope.

He hadn't put many trip wires along the front of the house as the gunman had always come in through the backyard. It didn't make sense that the gunman would saunter up to the front door of the house, but now he wasn't so sure.

Then it hit him. Binoculars. What if the light he'd glimpsed had been the reflection of the moonlight off a pair of binoculars?

The moment the possibility entered his mind, he heard the faint sound of the front door closing.

*No!* His pulse spiked with fear. Pulling his Sig Sauer from its holster, he lightly ran along the side of the house, keeping to the shadows. Sierra's barking and growling told him everything he needed to know.

The gunman had been hiding across the street, watching as he'd keyed in the code. Which meant the guy had already gained access to the house.

Scenarios flickered through his mind as he turned and ran back to the windows by the study. If he called 911, the Agoura Hills police department would send several squads to the scene, no doubt with full lights and sirens. The gunman was already inside the house and could easily hold Charlotte and the other women and children hostage.

Had the gunman watched Kaleb go outside? Or was the perp assuming he was in the house too?

He didn't know.

Anyone with military training would realize he'd be stationed outside, but he didn't think this gunman had that level of experience. Through the window in the study, Kaleb had a clear view of the alarm keypad. Not good, since the perp could have watched them enter the code from here. The green light indicated the alarm was not engaged. It would go off any minute, unless someone entered the code.

It was the opening he needed. Praying Sierra's barking would hide the sound of glass breaking, he hit the window with his elbow, punching through the glass. Then he cleared the glass fragments away with his arm. After unlocking the window, he lifted the sash and crawled inside. He managed to slide the window closed seconds before he caught the faint beeping of the alarm system being silenced.

Pain shot up his arm where the glass cut his skin, but he ignored it. Now that he was inside the house, he could hear the conversation going on in the main room.

"I told you to shut that dog up! Don't make me kill it!"

"I'm trying." Charlotte's voice was surprisingly calm. "Easy, Sierra. It's okay, girl. Shhh . . ."

Unfortunately, Kaleb knew Sierra wasn't going to be quiet. Not when her protective instincts were on full alert.

He'd given her the command to guard, and it was clear the dog was taking that direction to heart. Kaleb lightly ran to the study doorway, hoping the dog would calm down once she caught his scent.

Panic clawed up his throat. He couldn't bear the thought of Sierra being killed by this guy. *Please, Lord, please? Don't take Sierra from me . . .*

"It's okay, Sierra. We're okay." Charlotte's voice held a sense of urgency. "Be quiet, girl, please be quiet."

The dog abruptly stopped barking.

From his position, Kaleb couldn't get a good view of Charlotte or Sierra. But he did see the gunman standing with his back to the door. There was a dark stain along the upper side of his arm, likely blood from where he'd dinged him earlier. There was no doubt in his mind that this was the same man who'd shot at the safe house that first night and again earlier that day.

And he was now holding a gun trained on Charlotte and Sierra. With only a few feet between them, it wasn't likely this guy could miss.

Kaleb was close enough that he could probably take the guy out, but doing so could cause the gunman to reflexively fire his weapon. A risk he didn't dare take. He eased back from the doorway, sweeping his gaze around the study, looking for something to use as a diversion.

"Get to your feet, Charlotte," the guy said. "Come with me voluntarily and no one else needs to be killed."

"Okay, Jerry. But I'd feel better if you would put the gun down first."

"Yeah, that's not happening," Jerry responded. "Now move!"

Kaleb knew he was running out of time. There wasn't a doubt in his mind that Charlotte would go with Jerry to keep the rest of the residents safe. He found a small paper-weight on the desk and hurried back to the doorway.

Thankfully, Charlotte was still sitting on the sofa. Kaleb drew in a deep breath and lifted his weapon. Then he tossed the paperweight to the gunman's left, near the kitchen. He was holding his Sig Sauer with both hands by the time it landed, making a solid *thunk* as it hit the counter.

As he'd hoped, Jerry immediately looked that way, moving the muzzle of the gun in that direction too, giving Kaleb the opportunity to aim and fire.

The echo of the shot shattered the silence. His bullet hit its mark, sending Jerry stumbling backward against the door. A second gunshot followed, and Kaleb leaped forward, fearing Jerry had pulled the trigger.

Only, Jerry's body jerked again as if hit by a second bullet. That's when he realized Charlotte had the pillow in her lap, her own weapon trained on Jerry from underneath.

Jerry's eyes were wide with shock as the gun fell from his hand.

Kaleb came forward to kick the gun out of reach. Then he turned toward Charlotte, her eyes wide, her face pale as she stared at the man they'd both shot.

"I—had to stop him . . ." Her voice was barely a whisper.

"Yes, you did," he assured her. He dropped beside her on the sofa and pulled her close. "I'm so sorry. I should have realized what was going on . . ."

"Charlotte? Are you okay?"

He turned to look toward the stairs. Milly, Willow, and the other women were gathered there, no doubt woken by the gunfire.

"I called 911," Milly said. "The police will be here shortly."

"That's good, thanks, Milly." Kaleb smiled reassuringly.

"You may want to keep everyone upstairs, though, so we don't contaminate the crime scene. And to spare the kids from seeing something they shouldn't."

Like Jerry's dead body.

"We will." Milly turned and took charge. "Ladies, I need you all to return to your rooms. We'll talk to the police when they get here."

There was a murmur of protests before the women turned away to do as Milly asked.

"Is he dead?" Charlotte asked.

Kaleb looked at Jerry's body. There was no reason to leave Charlotte's side to check for a pulse. He could tell from here his bullet had struck the guy square in the chest, and Charlotte's bullet had gone into his abdomen. There was no sign of Jerry breathing, and his eyes were open and staring blindly out at nothing.

"I'm afraid so." He drew her closer. "I'm sorry, Charlotte. So sorry you were forced to shoot at him. I should have gotten to him first."

She sank against him, her body trembling in the aftermath of the situation. That and the adrenaline rush that came with shooting someone.

It was never easy. Not even for him as a SEAL. But less so for Charlotte.

"I didn't want to go with him." Her voice was muffled against his chest. "But I couldn't let him hurt anyone else either."

"I know." He pressed a kiss to the top of her head. He felt awful that she'd been forced into this position, firing her .38 in self-defense. "I wanted to spare you that, but I couldn't let you know I was behind you without tipping him off. I threw the paperweight as a diversion, hoping to distract him long enough for me to take him out."

She finally lifted her head to look up at him, her cheeks damp with tears. "I thought it was strange that Sierra stopped barking. Was that because of you?"

He reached out a hand to stroke Sierra, who was crowding against their legs. "I'm not sure. I prayed for God to spare her while hoping she'd pick up my scent." He used the pad of his thumb to lightly wipe away her tears. "I'm so glad you weren't hurt, Charlotte. If anything had happened to you . . ." He couldn't finish.

He loved her.

The realization washed over him, putting his entire life in perspective. He'd served his country with honor, and now that he was a civilian, God had brought him here. To Charlotte. And the others, to keep them safe.

There wasn't a doubt in his mind this was all part of God's plan.

Before he could say anything, though, he heard the wail of sirens. He gently eased away from Charlotte. "Stay here, I'll meet with the officers."

With Sierra hovering at his side, he holstered his gun, then opened the front door, using the edge of his jacket to protect fingerprint evidence. Stepping outside, he lifted his hands high when he saw every cop had his weapon drawn.

"My name is Kaleb Tyson, and I'm a retired Navy SEAL. There is a dead gunman inside, a man named Jerry Schubert who was shot in self-defense."

The officers glanced at each other. "Keep your hands high so we can see them," one of them shouted.

His hands were already up and within their line of vision, but he understood this was not something they encountered every day. Not in the posh suburb of Agoura Hills. "Call Detective Wales," he said loudly. "He knows the details of this situation."

A pair of officers approached him cautiously while another one made the call to the detective.

Kaleb laced his hands on his head, knowing the drill. "I have a Sig Sauer in my right hip holster and a MK 3 knife on the left."

The officers quickly took his weapons and then stepped back out of reach.

"Hey, Wales said he's legit," the cop near the squad said loudly. "Said there's been a gunman stalking this house for the past twenty-four hours."

It was longer than that, but Kaleb didn't bother to correct him.

"Wales wants us to preserve the crime scene until he gets here," the cop continued. "We need to set up a perimeter."

"You'll also want to station an officer at the house across the street," Kaleb said. "I believe Jerry was hiding there, watching the front door. He accessed the house by entering the key code, which he likely saw through binoculars. Then he silenced the alarm code once he was inside, getting that code through watching one of the other windows as well."

Again, the officers looked at each other questioningly before one of them nodded. "I'll go."

"Thank you." Kaleb slowly lowered his arms.

The officer who'd taken his weapons came up to stand beside him. "You want to explain what happened here tonight?"

"I'd rather wait until Detective Wales gets here. That way I only have to go through the story once."

The officer frowned. "Tell me anyway."

Kaleb suppressed a sigh, then started at the beginning. He hadn't gotten very far when the same ugly brown sedan pulled up and Wales emerged from behind the wheel.

"Tyson? Everyone okay?" the detective asked.

"Yes, except for the gunman. I'm sorry to say he's dead."

Wales didn't look surprised by the news, but then he glanced around. "You shot him inside the house?"

"Yes." Kaleb explained about the flash of light likely being binoculars and how he'd broken into the house through the study. "I hit him in the chest a second before Charlotte fired, landing a shot in his abdomen. He went down hard. You should know I heard him threaten to kill the other women if she didn't go with him." He hesitated, then added, "I believe his name is Jerry Schubert, and he's Charlotte's former boyfriend or fiancé, I am not sure which."

Wales eyebrows levered up. "She was abused by him?"

"Yes." Kaleb gestured to the house. "She can tell you the whole story herself. She told me he was in Minneapolis, recently married to someone new."

"I see." Wales turned toward the officers. "Get the crime scene techs out here. I want the house across the street checked for fingerprints as well as the front door here."

Kaleb followed Wales into the house where Charlotte was still sitting on the sofa as if afraid to move.

The danger was over, but he couldn't escape the terrible guilt. If only he'd have figured out what the flash had been sooner. And he should have taken care to hide the alarm code and key code from prying eyes. Not easy with so many people living there, but still failures that could have been prevented.

Charlotte shouldn't have been forced to shoot Jerry. Even from here, he could tell by the stark expression in her eyes that deep wounds had been left behind.

Wounds that he knew from personal experience would never fully heal.

---

SHE'D KILLED HIM.

Charlotte grappled with the fact that she'd killed Jerry. When he'd first come inside, she'd felt incapable of pulling the trigger. That there was no way she could shoot at a living, breathing person.

Then he'd silenced the alarm, somehow knowing the code. Then told her that if she went along with him willingly, he wouldn't kill anyone else. There had been a flicker of something in his gaze that made her think he hadn't been talking about the women and children upstairs.

But Darla? His wife? The woman she'd sent an anonymous letter to, warning of Jerry's temper and subsequent abuse? Oh yeah.

Instinctively, she'd suspected Jerry had killed Darla. It was the only reason she could think of that he'd come looking for her after all this time. It was typical of Jerry to blame everyone else for the things he'd done.

She avoided looking at Jerry's dead body. As much as she hated having pulled the trigger, she wasn't entirely sorry he was dead. Especially if he really had killed Darla, the way she believed.

Her attention was diverted from her thoughts when Kaleb and Detective Wales came inside the house.

"Charlotte? Are you okay?" Kaleb's gaze was full of concern.

"I didn't want to ruin the evidence." She glanced at the pillow in her lap, the gun she'd set on the sofa cushion beside her.

"It's okay," Detective Wales assured her. He came forward and put her .38 in a plastic evidence bag. "I've heard Tyson's side of the story, why don't you tell me yours?"

"I heard the key code being entered and thought Kaleb was coming inside. But it was Jerry, only he'd changed his appearance. He dyed his hair black and must have had something done to his nose and his cheekbones because his face was altered from what I remembered." She still couldn't figure out if Jerry had done that on purpose or if someone had punched him in the face, maybe both. "Oh, and he had a gun pointed at me."

"I kicked it away after he was shot," Kaleb added. "It's over there."

Wales nodded, his gaze holding hers. "What did he say?"

"He—uh, kept threatening to shoot the dog because she was barking and growling. Then he said if I came with him, he wouldn't have to kill anyone else. I—uh, had the impression he was talking about his wife, Darla." She reached out to touch Wales's hand. "You need to contact the Minneapolis police department, see if Darla Schubert is safe."

"I will," Wales agreed. "Then what happened?"

She thought back to those moments that seemed like a blur. "I had my gun under the pillow and had subtly pulled it onto my lap. There was a noise in the kitchen, and when Jerry looked that way, I shot him."

"I shot first," Kaleb interrupted. "I saw him fall back beneath the impact of the bullet."

She nodded slowly, the images replaying in her mind. It was sweet of Kaleb to take the blame, but she owned a piece of what had happened that night. "The women and children were sleeping upstairs, but our gunfire woke them up. I believe Milly called 911."

"I did," Milly called from the stairs.

"Okay, thank you." Wales turned toward Kaleb. "I need you and Charlotte to go in the other room while we gather evidence. Sounds like everything happened here in the main living area."

Kaleb nodded and reached down to help her up. A wave of dizziness hit, and she thought she might collapse. But Kaleb slid his arm around her waist, holding her upright.

"It's over," Kaleb whispered in a low voice. "He can't hurt you or anyone else ever again."

"I know." She allowed Kaleb to usher her to the dining room. Sierra followed as if unwilling to be away from Kaleb's side. She didn't blame the dog, she felt the same way. "I had no idea the gunman was Jerry." She looked up into Kaleb's dark eyes. "How did he find me? Through my anonymous letter to his wife?"

"Maybe," Kaleb agreed. "We'll learn more when Wales finds out what happened back in Minneapolis."

She nodded. "I hate knowing that the women and children were only in danger because of me."

"Because of Jerry," he corrected. "You didn't do this, Charlotte. Remember that, okay?"

"I'll try." Logically, she knew he was right. She wouldn't have blamed Willow or any of the other women if their abusers had come after them. "Thank you, Kaleb. For saving our lives."

"I wish I had done a better job of protecting you," he said with a frown.

"Don't say that. You did everything right. I should have reacted quicker when Sierra started to growl and bark." She shook her head. "I knew something was wrong. I just never expected . . ."

"Shh." Kaleb drew her close. "Let's not rehash what we both wish we had done differently but cherish this moment right here. God brought us together for a reason, Charlotte. He guided us to this place at this time. It was through God's grace that we worked together as a team, bringing down an evil man."

His words brought a sense of peace. "You're right, Kaleb. God was guiding us tonight. We prevailed because of Him."

"Exactly." His gaze searched hers for a long moment before he lowered his mouth. She could have stepped back to avoid his kiss, but she didn't.

Instead, she welcomed his kiss, reveled in his warm embrace. Their lips clung, then meshed. Instantly, the horrors of the night faded away as love welled from deep within.

She loved him. Loved everything about Kaleb with a depth she'd never felt before.

"Mom, Kaleb is kissing Miss Charlotte!"

Tommy's incredulous voice broke them apart. Charlotte blushed as she saw Willow and Tommy standing there, watching with interest. A hint of sadness flickered in Willow's gaze.

"Sorry to interrupt," Willow said. "Tommy insisted on seeing Kaleb to make sure he was not hurt."

"I'm fine, Tommy." Kaleb smiled down at the boy while keeping his arm around her waist. "So is Charlotte. The danger is over, there's no reason to be afraid."

"See, Tommy? I told you they were fine." Willow's gaze was apologetic.

"I had to see for myself," Tommy said. "Because us guys gotta stick together, right, Kaleb?"

"Right. But you need to listen to your mother, Tommy. She loves you and doesn't want you to be hurt."

"I know." Tommy shifted from one foot to the other. "Why were you kissing?"

Charlotte blinked at his blunt question.

"Because I love Charlotte," Kaleb said without missing a beat. "It's okay to kiss a lady as long as you are in love."

Love? She glanced at Kaleb, wondering if he felt the need to say that just to appease Tommy. But he gazed back at her, his dark brown eyes full of emotion.

"I love you, Charlotte, more than mere words can express. I know you've been through a difficult time, and you probably don't feel the same way, but I'm begging you to give us a chance."

"I—uh—" She tried to gather her scattered thoughts. "I have a safe house to run. I'm not sure how to make that work . . ."

"I would never ask you to give up your mission," he quickly interrupted. "I share your concern for women and children in abusive situations. I'd like to help, to be your partner." He hesitated, then added, "Unless this is your way of saying you don't feel the same way about me."

"No. I mean, yes." She was making a mess of this. "I love you too, Kaleb."

"You do?" Relief relaxed his features. "That's good to hear."

"Kaleb, I love you, but I don't know how to run a safe house with a man living on the premises. Not when the women who come there seeking safety are afraid of men."

"That's not really a problem," Willow spoke up from the doorway.

Charlotte flushed, not realizing Willow and Tommy were still standing there. And that Milly and several others had joined them.

"Willow is right," Milly said firmly. "These women are afraid of those who hurt them, not all men."

"And having a man protecting us is more important than what we might think we're afraid of," Willow added. "Not that we didn't feel safe with you, Charlotte. But having Kaleb nearby was even more reassuring."

"Agreed," Milly said with a smile. "Plus, you could put Willow in charge and maybe even open another safe house location. There's dozens of possibilities if you really think about it."

Charlotte glanced at Kaleb. She'd expected him to be nodding in agreement, but his gaze was focused solely on her.

"I want you to be comfortable with how things work out in the future, Charlotte," he said in a low voice. "I want to be a part of your life, part of the good work you're doing for others. But your opinion is the only one that matters."

She smiled, realizing that there was nothing to worry about. Kaleb would work with her, no matter what needed to be done. She reached up and drew his head down to hers. "I love you, Kaleb Tyson," she whispered before kissing him again.

He crushed her close, stealing her breath as he deepened their kiss. She clung to him for support, so lost in his love that she barely registered the smattering of applause coming from the group of women behind them.

Kaleb was right. She truly believed God had brought them together for a reason. By working together, she and Kaleb could do so much for the women and children who needed the safety and security of the women's shelter.

Losing herself in Kaleb's embrace, she felt God's loving light shining down upon them.

# EPILOGUE

They didn't get any sleep that night, but the following morning, Kaleb arranged for a charter bus to take the women and children back to their original safe house. The bloodstained rental house made it impossible to stay. And he knew he'd have to pay for the deep cleaning that would need to take place once the police released the scene.

Kaleb had learned from Detective Wales that Darla had been strangled to death over a month ago. From the evidence found at the scene, the Minneapolis police had named Jerry Schubert as a suspect. Especially upon finding the letter that Charlotte had sent warning Darla of Jerry's physical and emotional abuse.

From there, it seemed that Jerry's cop brother had helped protect Jerry from being caught. Then the idiot had gone a step further, getting Jerry connected with officers in Los Angeles, the postmark on the letter, who knew about the safe houses. Jerry had found Charlotte, then had plotted to get her back.

After they'd learned all of that, Detective Grimes had called to say he had Rodney Jones in custody. Blood matching Emma's had been found in his apartment, and he was being charged with her murder.

Kaleb couldn't deny he was glad to know both men wouldn't be hurting anyone ever again.

When a dark blue Jeep pulled up in front of the house, Kaleb belatedly remembered Hudson had driven all night to join him. He crossed over to meet his buddy.

"What happened?" Hudd asked with a frown. He emerged from the Jeep, followed closely by his male German shepherd, Echo.

"It's over," Kaleb said. He kept his gaze focused on Hudson's right eye as the left one was a glass prosthesis. "The gunman is dead, and no one has been hurt. I'm sorry I dragged you and Echo down here."

Hudd shrugged, taking in the scene. A few police officers were still present, even though Jerry Schubert's body had been taken away and most of the evidence had been collected. "Glad you're safe."

"The gunman turned out to be Charlotte's ex-fiancé," Kaleb explained. "We just learned he recently killed his wife, Darla, back in Minneapolis. The cops have been looking for him throughout the state of Minnesota, but he was here in Los Angeles searching for Charlotte. Turns out his cop brother helped him find her." A fact Kaleb intended to pursue to the fullest extent of the law. No cop should be using official resources to help his brother find a woman he'd formerly abused.

"Got what he deserved," Hudd said.

Kaleb couldn't disagree, although he still felt guilty for letting the guy get inside the house. Failures that would stick with him for a long time. "Come on, I want you to meet Charlotte Cambridge." He tugged on Hudd's arm. "She's an amazing woman."

Hudd hung back. "No need. Gotta go."

"Charlotte?" At his shout, Charlotte glanced over from the bus. Seeing him with Hudd, she hurried over to join them. "I want you to meet one of my SEAL teammates, Hudson Foster. He was the rock of our SEAL team, helping to cover my six more times than I can count. Hudd, this is the woman I love, Charlotte Cambridge."

Hudd nodded. "Nice to meet you."

"I'm honored to meet you, Hudson." Charlotte acted as if she didn't notice his glass eye as she smiled brightly at his buddy. "I hope at some point to meet all of Kaleb's teammates."

"You'll meet them at our wedding," Kaleb told her.

Hudson cocked a brow as Charlotte gaped at him. "Did you just ask me to marry you?"

"That wasn't a proper marriage proposal," he said hastily, mentally smacking himself upside the head. His exhaustion must be getting to him. "I know you need time to get used to the idea."

"Yes," Charlotte said.

He blinked as the corner of Hudd's mouth quirked in a rare smile. "Yes, what?"

"I don't need time to get used to the idea," she said. "When you're ready to ask me properly, the answer is yes."

He wished he had an engagement ring, but that didn't stop him from going down on one knee, cradling her hand between both of his. "Charlotte, I love you with all my heart and soul. Will you please do me the honor of becoming my wife?"

She blushed and nodded. "Yes, Kaleb. I'd love to marry you."

Kaleb stood and pulled her into his arms, swinging her in a wide circle. Then he realized Hudd had turned away and was heading for his Jeep. "I love you, too, but wait here." He released Charlotte and ran to catch up with Hudd. "Hey, where are you going?"

"Idaho." Hudd opened his car door and gestured for Echo to jump up. The large German shepherd nimbly landed in the passenger seat.

"Do you need help? What's going on in Boise, Idaho, anyway?" Kaleb asked, feeling frustrated. Hudd had only just arrived, and now he was clearly determined to leave.

Hudd shook his head, then hesitated, before answering, "My past." Without explaining anything more, his teammate slid behind the wheel, closed the door, and started the Jeep.

Moments later, Hudson was gone as quickly as he'd arrived.

Kaleb blew out a breath, wishing he could follow him. But the scene here was such that he couldn't just take off, at least not yet. Even though Jerry was dead, he needed to make sure Charlotte and the rest of the women were safely transported back to their original safe house and to ensure the windows had been repaired. It would also take time to match the DNA from the hat and the blood to Jerry's, although the boot print he'd found was enough to convince him they had the right man.

Detectives Wales and Grimes believed that too.

Charlotte came up to stand beside him. "Will Hudson be okay?"

"I hope so." Kaleb reluctantly turned away from the Jeep's retreating taillights. He gathered Charlotte close and buried his face against her short, silky dark hair. He was truly blessed to have found a woman like Charlotte to share the rest of his life with.

He could only hope and pray Hudson would find whatever he was looking for.

I HOPE you enjoyed Kaleb and Charlotte's story in *Sealed with Honor*. Are you ready for Hudson and Kendra's story in *Sealed with Justice*? Click here!

# DEAR READER

I hope you are enjoying my Called to Protect series. I'm having fun writing about these Navy SEAL heroes who are struggling with the pain of losing a teammate while trying to adapt to civilian life. The least I could do was help them find love. I hope you enjoyed Kaleb and Charlotte's path to their happily ever after.

I'm hard at work finishing up Hudson and Kendra's story in *Sealed with Justice*. My goal is to have all six books finished before the end of the year, although I do have several books under contract with Harlequin too. I'm writing as fast as I can.

I adore hearing from my readers! I can be found through my website at https://www.laurascottbooks.com, via Facebook at https://www.facebook.com/LauraScottBooks, Instagram at https://www.instagram.com/laurascottbooks/, and Twitter at https://twitter.com/laurascottbooks. Also, take a moment to sign up for my monthly newsletter, all subscribers receive a free novella, *Starting Over*, that is not available for purchase on any platform.

Until next time,

Laura Scott

PS: If you're interested in a sneak peek of *Sealed with Justice*, I've included the first chapter here.

# SEALED WITH JUSTICE

## Chapter One

Kendra Pickett gently massaged her injured shoulder as she walked down the street in her old neighborhood located in Eagle, a suburb to the northeast of Boise, Idaho. The April weather was cool as dusk hovered on the horizon. She was on a paid leave from her job as a trauma critical care nurse at a large hospital in Portland, Oregon. The past two years had been rough, first filing for divorce from her husband, then losing her young daughter to cancer. Finding God had been the only thing that had kept her from driving her car into the ocean, and she was grateful for her church friends.

Being forced to stay home had left her at loose ends, and she'd decided a change of scenery was in order. Her dad still lived in Eagle, and visiting with him was no hardship.

Yet coming home brought troubled memories to the surface. Losing her daughter to cancer had been the worst experience of her life, her divorce from Dr. Don Walker, cheating surgeon extraordinaire being a welcome relief.

The second worst experience of her life was when Zoey

Barkley, her best friend in high school, had gone missing. The seventeen-year-old had been found twelve hours later in a cave on the other side of the creek, strangled to death. Twenty years later, Zoey's murder remained unsolved.

At least officially, it remained unsolved. Kendra knew Zoey's former boyfriend, Hudson Foster had killed her, but apparently the Eagle police didn't have any evidence to prove it. Hudson had claimed he was innocent, but everyone knew he had been in other fights, granted, mostly related to defending his drunken mother.

Even so, there was no denying Hudson had a temper. Plus, he'd left the state to join the military right after graduation. Running away, she'd thought sourly. To her knowledge, he hadn't been back since.

It irked her that Hudson had gotten away with killing Zoey. It wasn't right, and while she knew there was no statute of limitations on murder, it wasn't likely that new evidence would come to light now, twenty years later.

Yet that hadn't stopped her from asking questions around town, starting with the police station. So far, her efforts had been met with disdain. Feeling restless, she'd walked from her dad's house down to the river, where she and Zoey had often hung out after school because Zoey hadn't wanted to go home. Zoey's dad had been the Eagle Chief of Police back then, and her brother Andrew had bossed Zoey around, making her do all the cooking and cleaning after their mother had passed away. As if those chores were beneath him.

Zoey and Kendra had enjoyed sitting at the creek. They would sit beneath the shelter of large trees, and in the winter, they'd often hide out in the cave.

The same cave where Zoey's body had been found.

Kendra turned off the main road, heading over the hilly

terrain to the creek. Maybe she'd been silly to come here at night, but she wasn't afraid.

Nothing could hurt her anymore, not after she'd lost Olivia. Sweet, sweet, Olivia.

Two years, felt like another lifetime. She was grateful for the darkness as tears pricked her eyes. Brushing them away, she fought back the memories. She'd cried more in those months after losing Olivia than she had in her entire life.

Tears wouldn't bring Olivia back. Zoey either. They were both with God now, along with her mother, Grace.

Kendra stood for a moment at the water's edge, wishing she could talk to Zoey one last time. Zoey would have been there for her during Olivia's year-long illness. Her friend would have supported her during the divorce too.

"What happened to you, Zoey?" Her voice echoed over the water.

"I've been asking that very same thing," a deep male voice said.

Kendra spun around. She was so badly startled that she tripped over her own feet and hit the ground hard. Then she scrabbled backward to put distance between herself and the man and dog she could barely see standing within the shadow of the trees.

"Who's there?" she asked, squinting through the darkness. So much for thinking she couldn't be scared. Her heart was pounding so fast she thought she'd suffer an acute MI.

"It's me. Hudd and my dog, Echo." A tall, muscular man stepped out from the shadows with a large tan and brown German shepherd at his side. She gaped in surprise at seeing the man she'd just been thinking about.

"When did you get here?" Stupid question, but her brain wasn't firing on all cylinders.

"Here at the creek? Or to Eagle?"

"Both." She rose to her feet and crossed her arms defensively over her chest. Her shoulder hurt worse after hitting the ground, and she gritted her teeth against the pain. Lifting her chin, she stared at him. As a critical care nurse, she'd dealt with her fair share of arrogant surgeons. She'd learned to stand her ground, especially when it came to making sure her patients got the care they needed. Just because Hudson Foster seemed bigger, taller, and stronger than she remembered, that didn't mean she was going to back down. Although the dog was enough to give her pause. For all she knew, he'd trained the animal to attack humans on command. "You have some nerve asking what happened to Zoey when you're the only one who knows the truth."

"Still beating that drum, huh, Kendra?" He shrugged and glanced off into the distance for a moment before turning back to face her. "I didn't kill her. Had no reason to."

His calm statement caught her off guard. Twenty years ago, he'd seemed desperate for people to believe him. Now, Hudson Foster appeared as if he couldn't care less what people thought.

"Getting angry about Zoey dumping you and attending homecoming with Tristan Donahue is reason enough."

"She tell you that?" Hudd shrugged again, his hand resting on the top of his dog's head. "I was glad she went with Tristan. I had no intention of going to homecoming anyway."

Kendra scowled, wondering if he'd spun this story over the years to cover his tracks. She reached up to massage her left shoulder, praying she hadn't injured it worse. "Whatever. I know the truth."

"You know nothing." For the first time, the hint of anger

she remembered from twenty years ago flashed in his eyes. Then it was gone, and he waved a hand toward the residential area behind them. "Echo and I will walk you home."

"No thanks." The last person she wanted to be seen with was Hudson Foster. She turned and was about to retrace her steps when Hudson unexpectedly emerged beside her, moving with the speed and stealth of a cougar. The dog had also moved without making a sound. She almost fell, but he grabbed her arm, holding her steady.

"We'll walk you home." He said the words as if they were a forgone conclusion.

"I'd rather go alone." She shook off his hand, secretly surprised at his gentle touch. She'd expected brute force from a man with muscles on top of muscles.

Hudson's current physique, even at the age of thirty-nine, made her ex look like a wimp.

And it was different from the way Hudson had looked twenty years ago. Obviously being in the military had changed him. Not that she was remotely interested in a man she knew had murdered her best friend.

"No." Hudson's voice made the hairs on the back of her neck stand up. It was all too familiar to the way Don had treated her at the end of their marriage.

"Yes. Please leave me alone." She took a step away from him at the exact moment a shot rang out.

"Down!" Hudson reacted instinctively, reaching over to pull her down, placing his body over hers while pulling something from his waistband. The dog growled and hovered beside them. With her face plastered against the ground, she couldn't tell what was going on, until she heard more gunfire. Much louder.

Coming from Hudson? Was he armed too?

What on earth had she gotten herself into?

SURPRISINGLY, the gunfire had come from the direction of the residential neighborhood. Hudd couldn't pinpoint an exact location, although he did his best to sweep his good eye over the area.

After he'd returned fire, he thought he'd heard a car engine, possibly the gunman leaving the scene. His hearing was more acute now that he'd lost the vision in his left eye. Their last SEAL op had gone sideways, and he'd been hit in eye with a piece of debris. Thankfully, his right eye had been spared, and he wasn't completely blind.

"Easy, Echo." The dog calmed but still looked alert. Hudd stayed exactly where he was, covering Kendra's slim body with his, refusing to assume they were safe. If he'd been the gunman, he'd have taken cover and waited for them to stand up before trying again.

Not that Hudson would have missed the first time. He'd been one of the better marksmen of their team, second only to Dallas.

After several long moments, Kendra pushed at him. "Let me up. I can't breathe!"

He knew his weight could be crushing her, so he shifted to the side, but he didn't let up. "Stay down. I don't know if the shooter is still out there."

"You're the shooter," she accused. "I heard your gun go off."

"In self-defense." He was getting mighty tired of defending himself. Kendra had made it clear she thought he was guilty of killing Zoey, and normally that wouldn't matter.

Except for some reason, it did. Especially coming from Kendra, a girl he'd secretly crushed on back in high school.

Only Kendra had dated Corey Robinson, the quarter-back of the football team.

Whatever. What did that matter? No reason to dwell on stuff that happened twenty years ago. He continued scanning the area, searching for any sign of the gunman. Finally, he stood and offered a hand to Kendra. To his surprise, she took it. He pulled her to her feet, then quickly released her. He didn't holster his weapon, preferring to keep it in hand. "Heel, Echo."

The dog came to sit at his side.

"I don't understand what happened," she said with a frown. "Is someone trying to kill you?"

"I'm not sure if I was the target or you were." He thought back to those last seconds before hearing the gunshot. "You moved away from me, remember? I think the bullet passed between us."

"Me?" Kendra's jaw dropped. "That's impossible. I've only been here two days, why would someone shoot at me?"

"I don't know." Hudd didn't like the situation one bit. He'd been in Eagle for almost a week, minus two days of traveling back to Los Angeles and back, but he'd made sure not to be seen around town.

To be honest, he wasn't sure why he'd announced his presence to Kendra. If he had stayed silent, she'd have never seen him and Echo.

Although if he hadn't shown himself, she might already be dead.

He grimaced. This was why you didn't play the what-if game. Better to focus on the situation as is. No point in trying to change the past.

"This way." He pulled her toward the trees where he'd been crouched when she'd arrived at the creek. Echo came with him, staying close to his left side. It was his vulnerable side, after he'd lost vision in that eye. He focused on Kendra. "Are you sure there isn't anyone after you? A boyfriend, husband, or jilted lover?"

She stared up at him. "My ex-husband left me for another woman, no reason for him to come after me. Besides, he's in Portland, Oregon."

"And no other men in your life?" Why he was pressing he had no clue.

She shook her head. "No. And I don't see why anyone would shoot at me. I think you must be the target. The guy missed because he's probably just a lousy shot and couldn't see clear in the darkness."

"Motive?" Hudson drawled.

"I'm sure you've made enemies over the years." She waved a hand. "And showing up here after all this time is just asking for trouble. The entire town believes you killed Zoey twenty years ago. My guess is that someone is trying to make you pay for that."

"Like Zoey's brother, Andrew, or her father? George retired from his job as police chief two years ago but still actively hunts, and her brother, Andrew, is the new chief of police. I doubt either one of them would have missed me."

Kendra opened her mouth, then closed it again. Then she shivered, and he had the ridiculous urge to wrap his arm around her. It almost made him smile to imagine her punching him in the stomach or slapping his face in response.

Almost.

Hudd hadn't smiled or laughed in the months since being medically discharged from the navy minus one eye while suffering terrible migraine headaches. If not for Echo, he figured he'd be dead by now.

"We can't just hide here." Kendra sounded annoyed. "I need to get home. My dad will wonder where I am."

He already knew Kendra had come home for a few weeks and was staying with her father at the house she grew up in. He'd kept his ears open while staying out of sight. It was surprising what the good citizens of Eagle discussed when they didn't know anyone was listening.

But now wasn't the time to tell her everything he knew. Including the murmurings of why people were asking about a twenty-year-old cold case.

"I need you to stay here while I check out the area to make sure the gunman isn't still hiding nearby." He stared down at her and mustered all the politeness he could find. "Kendra, will you please stay here for me? I really don't want anything to happen to you."

"Again, you're assuming the gunman was after me." Her tone lacked conviction as if she might be realizing the second possibility wasn't something to brush off so easily. "Yes, I'll wait here."

"Thank you." He gently positioned her up against the thickest tree truck. "Stay right here until I return. Echo, guard." The dog sat, his large ears perked forward. "Good boy."

"Oh, for Pete's sake . . . hey, where did you go?" The last words were said in a hushed whisper.

Hudd didn't answer as he'd already left the clearing beneath the trees to move over the rocky, hilly terrain. The sound of water rushing through the creek helped cover the sound of his footsteps. Despite his large size, his SEAL training had taught him how to move silently, blending in with the environment.

Every few steps, he paused to listen. He didn't hear anything other than the muted traffic and the occasional door slamming from the residential neighborhood beyond the hill. It was a far cry from the abandoned shack he'd grown up in on the outskirts of town.

It didn't take him long to clear the area. When he was satisfied the gunman was gone, he returned to Kendra and Echo.

"I never heard you!" Her tone carried a hint of accusation. "How did you do that?"

"Training." He gave Echo the hand signal to come, and the dog trotted over. "The area is clear. Are you ready to go?"

"Yes." He was glad Kendra didn't bother to argue about his plan to escort her home. The gunshot had obviously shaken her. And with good reason.

The more he thought about it, the more he was convinced Kendra was the gunman's intended target. "Might be better for you to head back to Portland."

"What?" She frowned at him. "Why would I do that?"

"To be safe." He hesitated, then asked, "Have you been asking questions about Zoey's murder since you've been home?"

Her eyes narrowed. "Did you hear that from someone in particular?"

He didn't respond.

After a full minute, she sighed. "Yes, I went to the Eagle police station to ask if they'd solved her murder. I was able to speak to Roger, one of the officers on duty, who told me the case was still open, but no one was actively pursuing it."

That much he'd gathered for himself based on the rudimentary internet search he'd done and the bits of conversations he'd overheard. Still, he remained silent, waiting for her to continue.

"I may have suggested that I planned to check out our

old hangouts to see if I could find out anything." She waved a hand. "But that was mostly just talk on my part. I didn't really think I'd be able to find anything. Besides, even if I did, who would care? Unless—wait a minute, you can't seriously think the killer is still living here."

"Why not?"

"I don't know." She sounded exasperated. "Most people don't stick around Eagle forever. They move closer to Boise or out of state."

"We did, yes. But not everyone. Zoey's family is still here and so are a few of our former classmates." Hudd frowned, thinking about what she'd said. "I heard that someone was asking questions about Zoey's murder, but I didn't realize you were the source."

She kicked at a rock. "Seems to me the Eagle police department should have continued to investigate. I can't imagine there's a ton of crimes keeping them busy."

He felt compelled to agree with her on that front. Eagle had never been a hotbed of crime, outside of the usual drugs, alcohol abuse, petty theft kind of thing. Zoey's murder had been huge, and Police Chief George Barkley had sworn to bring the perpetrator to justice.

Only he never had.

Not that the guy hadn't tried everything possible to convince Hudson to confess to the crime. The chief had kept Hudson in the box for hours on end, forcing him to repeat his story over and over. Until Hudson wised up and asked for a lawyer.

Still, Barkley had kept him in jail overnight claiming it was too late to get a lawyer. By the morning, though, the police had reluctantly let him go.

The only alibi he had at the time was his mother who'd been drunk as usual. Which wouldn't have held up in a court of law if there had been any other evidence to tie him to the crime.

Thankfully, there wasn't.

Hudd knew that was because he didn't kill Zoey. Although he'd kept expecting to get arrested again, despite the lack of evidence. And after he'd finally graduated from high school, he'd gone to the Boise armed services office and signed up to join the navy. He'd told the recruiter that he wanted to be a Navy SEAL, and the guy had smiled and nodded.

*That's a fine goal, son, but you gotta understand only the toughest men of the bunch get through BUD/S training.*

The recruiter had been right about that. Getting through BUD/S training had been the hardest thing he'd ever done. Kaleb was his swim buddy, the two of them leaning on each other to get through the program.

Hudd had given twenty years of his life to the navy. Unlike Kaleb, he hadn't tried to sustain a marriage throughout his deployments overseas. Being alone had suited him just fine. He didn't regret the path he'd chosen except maybe that last op that had claimed the life of their teammate, Jaydon Rampart.

"If you didn't kill Zoey, then who did?" Kendra's question broke into his thoughts.

"Beats me." He didn't bother to reiterate his innocence. "I've often wondered if it wasn't one of the football players. Maybe one of the guys who wanted Zoey but couldn't have her."

"Come on, really? I can't believe you're accusing my old boyfriend or one of his close friends of killing Zoey. That's ridiculous."

"Is it?" He'd personally never cared for any of the guys,

they'd always acted as if they were better than everyone else.

Especially him.

Coach Donahue had tried to convince him to play, as he could run fast, but Hudd had declined. Not just because of the way the other guys treated him but because he had to work two jobs after school. Heaven knew his mother couldn't hold a job.

"I know they weren't always nice to you, Hudson," she admitted. "But they weren't bad guys. Just a little too cocky for their own good."

That was putting it mildly. "And they were also the least likely to be considered a serious suspect by Chief Barkley, as his son was part of the group. They were all at some party from what I remember."

She didn't have a quick response to that, and they walked in silence for a few moments. Then she asked, "Where are you staying?"

"Does it matter?"

She stopped and turned to look at him. They were in the residential neighborhood now, and the streetlights illuminated her features. He had to admit, Kendra was even more beautiful than she had been twenty years ago. Her blonde hair wasn't as long, she wore it in a chin-length bob, but the style suited her. Her dark eyes seemed to draw him into their depths. "I'm just making polite conversation. Are you always so prickly?"

"Yeah." He glanced at Echo who was looking up at him as if trying to figure out what was going on. "I'm staying at the shack out in the woods, believe it or not it's still there even though my mom passed away ten years ago."

"Your old house? But it's . . ." Her voice trailed off.

"Barely standing? Doesn't have electricity or running

water? I know, but it's not as bad as some places I've stayed in." He'd take the old shack over the desert of Afghanistan any day.

"But—why? Do you need money? I can loan you some."

The rusty croaking sound coming from his throat was laughter. It surprised him more than it did her. "No, I have money."

Kendra was staring at him oddly, not unlike Echo, then shook her head and shrugged. He could tell she was thinking he had more than a few screws loose in the old noggin.

And maybe he did.

"How long are you staying?" she asked.

It was a good question. One of the many reasons he'd gone to the old shack rather than getting a motel room was that he preferred to come and go as he pleased. Especially important when a bad migraine hit.

He wasn't sure why he'd come back to Eagle in the first place. To face the memories of his mother? To prove to Barkley that he'd made something of himself?

To clear his name?

None of that really mattered. He could have easily left town early the next morning without anyone even realizing he was there.

It occurred to him that whoever had taken that shot at Kendra may have caught a glimpse of his face. If so, there was no reason to skulk around.

And more reason for him to stay, especially if Kendra was in danger.

"Hudson?" Kendra prodded.

"Three weeks." He glanced at her. "That's how long you're planning to stay, right?"

She looked taken aback. "Why does that matter?"

"You poked the sleeping bear, Kendra. You asked questions about Zoey's murder and made it clear you were going to search for answers." He wanted to shake some sense into her. "Haven't you figured out yet that you're in danger? The gunfire was intentional. I'm staying until I can figure out what is going on."

She gaped at him, then shivered again. As if on cue, bright headlights came out of the darkness, heading straight toward them. "Go, Echo!" Thankfully, the dog lurched to the side. Hudson grabbed Kendra, swinging her out of harm's way just as the edge of the car's bumper clipped his left knee, sending pain zinging through him. He managed to stay on his feet, but just barely.

His stupid peripheral vision sucked, or he could have avoided the car altogether. Unfortunately, by the time he spun around to find the vehicle responsible, the taillights were gone.

Two attempts to hurt or kill Kendra in less than two hours?

Not good.